D1827590

QUILAQ

REBECCA BURNS

For Al, Tom, Val, Mags

QUILAQ

Stokeland. It sits at a fork between two roads, one a thick, commercial highway bedevilled by ice for ninety percent of the year; the other a stripped, frozen weave of a road, impassable for ten months out of twelve and huddled beneath wedges of brilliant white snow. It is a wonder that Stokeland has any inhabitants at all; but it does, over a hundred souls.

Angie Barker is one. She sits in Shay's, Stokeland's only bar, watching the snow come again. It is just before lunch and a few townsfolk have made it in as well, their snow mobiles parked beside each other outside. They have come for the steamed moosemeat and sourdough, and some will chase it down with whiskey; Yukon Jack if they can afford it. Angie has cleaned the bar, ready for them, rinsing out the dirty glasses left from the night before and sweeping the sticky carpet, musky with sweat and the urgency of payday. Men come to the bar and spend their money from trapping or the zinc mines, as soon as they make it. They leave dull fingerprints on the pool table and the shiny surface of the bar, grubby reminders that they have yet to make enough to leave and head south where it is warmer.

Angie is thirty-nine and has been for a number of years. She is too heavy and her skin is too blotched for her to be anything other than a functional barmaid; the trappers and miners do not come into Shay's to see her, only to drink beer. She hasn't had to slap a hand away from her breasts for over six months. Not even after Ray Sullivan's divorce party. He'd been wanting to leave Wanda for an age and she finally let him after finding out he'd been seeing a stripper over in Tramper's Creek, where he tried to trade with the Inuit.

Shay's Bar had been packed the night of the divorce party. Jackie and Connor, men who worked down Stokeland's zinc mine and were never apart, hugged a table, swaying together. Others, faces she couldn't place, beamed over lines of shots. Shay's Bar pulsed and throbbed the night Ray Sullivan's divorce came through. By the time Angie stepped outside for a smoke, her shirt was damp from the unexpected exercise of running between kegs and optics.

In a roundabout way, Angie thinks as she wipes the bar, Ray's divorce has led to her being here, right this moment, waiting for one particular fellow to show. Today is her day off; she doesn't have to be in. She could have stayed in her room above the bar, where a stove keeps ice at bay and she could watch *Days of Our Lives* on repeat. Instead she is passing the time, sweeping floors that have already been swept and washing glasses that are already clean, waiting for Gerry the Gin to make an appearance.

"I don't actually like gin, but it's a thing that's stuck." That had been the night of Ray's party. Gerry the Gin had traded his furs to the Inuits that day and, like too many Stokelanders, had come to drink away his money before being driven back into the snow to snare more animals. His eyes had the sunken, overbright look of someone pinned into an addled, swilled-in-beer way of life, and the breath coming off him was foul. Angie had hung back at the bar, nudging the stubs of whiskey to him. But Gerry's shirt was clean and he still had a rough edge of an accent. It was enough to intrigue, in the washed-up room.

"That so? Nickname like that and you don't like gin." Angie nodded conversationally but still kept back from the fetid plumes drifting from the man's mouth. "Well, what else could it be?"

"Nickname? Hell, I don't know. Why does a man need a nickname anyway? Foxes and hares I skin couldn't give a tuppenny fuck what I'm called."

"Right," and Angie was about to move away, recognising the tipping point all men reached when booze had sloshed around in their stomachs for long enough.

"When'd you get here?" Gerry the Gin asked.

"When did I move to Stokeland?" Angie paused with her hand resting on a pump and thought hard. Santa Monica had been her home for the first thirty years, then Vancouver, with a man. That hadn't worked out and he'd left her with a cracked rib and venereal disease. Bar jobs, drifting north. Then Stokeland. "Can't remember, exactly. Five, six years, maybe."

"Can't remember either." Gerry winked and downed the shot of whiskey. "Left Skye in the forties, that much I do know."

"Skye?"

"The Isle of Skye. My dad was torpedoed at the end of 1944. Nothing else for my mother to do but start again somewhere. Canada as good a place as any."

Someone shouted at that point, Angie remembered, and a glass had smashed. Paul Shay, owner of the bar and a definite non-taker of bullshit, swore loudly and marched round to where Ray Sullivan and his friends were shuffling their feet. Angie watched, their heads bobbing, slurred promises given. A brush appeared from somewhere and a chastened man began sweeping.

Gerry the Gin chuckled into his glass. "Aye, Stokeland is a good a place as any." And then, "unless I were to ever find Quilaq."

Wiping a cloth over a beer tap as she waits for Gerry to show, Angie remembers how she felt when he said that strange word. It was as though someone rubbed an ice cube behind her belly-button: her stomach instantly began to ache, although the sensation was not exactly unpleasant. Quilaq. A word she somehow knew but had never said out-loud before. *Qu-il-ack.* And then, the night of Ray's party the cold in her stomach seemed to spread and she felt swollen with a longing to find out more, to understand, to know about Quilaq. But Gerry the Gin had fallen asleep, propped against the bar, and then he left.

So Angie now waits for him to appear again, so she can hear him say that word again. What does it mean? Is it a place? *Quilaq*.

And here he is again, Gerry the Gin. Angie has been waiting for him most of the morning, and finally sees him through the window of Shay's Bar, his form braced against the snow, arms wrapped around his body in resignation as he climbs down from his battered old truck, which looks incongruous next to the snow mobiles. He tramps towards the door. A blast of cold air, white flakes skidding haphazardly across the floor, and the man is inside. It's been a week since Ray Sullivan's party and Gerry has been trapping again.

When Gerry first said that word, the night of Ray's divorce party, Angie thought she'd misheard, or he really had toppled into the space laid bare by booze, the space where words make no sense. *Quilaq*. That wasn't a word.

But he said it again and his face took on a dreamy yet *clear* kind of expression that pinned Angie to the floor.

"Quilaq. The Inuits say it's a real place. A city in the clouds. Sometimes I reckon I seen it.

Shadows, ken. And the smells. Baking. Meat, roasting." Gerry's eyes closed softly. He smiled. "Shangri-La. You never heard the stories?"

She has been waiting to see him all week. The night of Ray's party, a moment after Gerry spoke, someone else had broken another glass and Paul Shay had started shouting. He was intolerant of breakages: glass was expensive to buy in Stokeland. Angie had to come from behind the bar to smooth things over and, when she was done, Gerry had folded into a heap on his barstool, a mozzarella thread of drool sliding down his arm. He had left soon after, blundering out into the night.

And now here he is, after seven long days spreading the length of his weight onto the snow, setting his snares so he can catch ptarmigan. Angie has spent that time with the word thrumming through her brain. *Quilaq*. When she cleaned the beer pumps. *Quilaq*. When she cooked up vats of chilli for the regulars. *Quilaq*. When she tried to sleep in her narrow bed, the television blinking out rolls of grey static.

Quilaq. It seems to speak to a part of her that she has tucked away so deeply she has forgotten it existed. It cracks open a compressed vault, allowing other memories to flow out: egg custard, the smell of rose water on fresh towels. The crease of her grandmother's neck. With the scent of the old lady's talcum powder in her nose, Angie searched for Gerry the Gin's face each night amongst the men propping up Shay's Bar, disappointment when he didn't show folding her stomach into a hot crush.

Now, after a long week, the old man crunches into Shay's Bar and peels back his wet coat. His bones protrude from his pale skin and he has the look of hunger Angie has seen on other men who spend too long on their own. He pulls himself up onto a stool and raises an eyebrow when she pushes a plate of chilli across the bar.

"In all my years, a woman has never given me food freely," he says.

"I want to talk about Quilaq," Angie replies. She turns away and reappears with two shots of whiskey.

Gerry whistles when he sees them. "You really do."

"It's just – I haven't heard the word before, I'm sure. But then I must have. Since you said it, I've not been able to think of anything else."

Gerry says nothing until he has cleared his plate and knocked back the first shot of Yukon Jack. He breathes out heavily, gales of spiced foulness billowing into Angie's face. She does not step back, though, and grips the beer pumps.

"I haven't eaten for over a day," and Gerry accepts an offered cigarette. "That was mighty welcome."

Angie shrugs. They smoke, odd companions for a cold, snow-bitten afternoon.

"Most folk round here will have heard of Quilaq," Gerry says, eventually. "But they'll likely think it's a story. Stuff you tell a kiddie at bedtime. You know. Like the big bad wolf or the witch. Those kinds of tales."

"You didn't talk the other night as though you thought it was a tale," Angie says.

Gerry shrugs. "I spend too long out on the tundra. Sleeping on the ground, dirt for a pillow. Earth and moss in my mouth when I wake up."

"But what about the Inuits? You said they believe Quilaq is real."

"Girl, why do you want to know so much?"

To which, Angie does not have an answer. She cannot unlock the ravel of her tongue to smooth out a straight, linear answer: the truth – that Quilaq makes her think of her grandmother's house, the one place she felt safe – sounds crazy. She can imagine a cautious look coming over Gerry's face, falling shutter-like over his eyes. She can see him edge carefully to the door, waving away the offer of another drink or smoke.

So instead she picks up a cloth and begins wiping down the bar. "I thought I knew most of the places round here, is all."

Gerry studies her for a long moment, rheumy eyes leaking down his cheeks. The glare off the snow can be eviscerating; Angie does not venture outside without her sunglasses. But crowsfeet around Gerry's eyes show he wears no glasses and hunts his animals with a screwed-up face, a grimace against the balls of fur and feather giving him a livelihood. He peers at Angie in silence until her cheekbones ache with keeping still.

"Yeah, the folks I meet believe it's a real place." Gerry accepts another cigarette. "Not like *our* kind of real, ken. Not like being-on-a-map real."

"What kind of real, then?"

"I don't know. Look, this old native I see from time to time. One of the Inuits who live beyond the Kirk Straits, amongst the caribou. Well, you get this fellow drunk enough, or cold enough, and he'll tell you about it." Gerry glances at the whorls of snow gathering pace outside the window. "Put a frozen man by a fire and his mouth will warm up with his soul. He's told me things about this place, Quilaq. The way it's timeless."

"Timeless?"

"It was hard to understand, ken. I don't talk much in their way and he knew only bits and pieces of our way. But that's what he meant. The years don't matter there."

Angie sighs and places a gathering hand over her face. The trapper made no sense.

Chilli dries in the matting of Gerry the Gin's beard and Angie resists the urge to lean across the bar with her cloth and wipe it away. She wonders if he has ever known a woman.

As he pokes an overlong fingernail into his ear and twists it around, leisurely, she doubts it. She doesn't look at the smear of yellow on his skin when he places his hand back on the bar. The clock above the pool table clicks around to two; dedicated drinkers, the ones who take it seriously, will be in soon. The anchor that has looped around Angie the past week seems to shift, and her mind turns to barrels and optics, checking she has enough to see her through to the evening when Paul will show up. That word, the one she has been unable to leave alone – the one she has returned to all week, like a bird to a nest – that word has gone. It had been something strange. Quiller? Quebec?

She once had a classmate in high school who moved to Quebec...and Angie is off, mind wandering lightly, opening doors somewhere. She gazes at Gerry, who gazes back at her. She wonders where he's gotten his chilli from.

And then the bar door opens and someone steps inside. A whorl of snow accompanies them, funnelling around the figure, wafting long skirts and laying waste to Angie's clean, mopped floor. It is Hettie Neil and, before she even speaks, Angie knows she is looking for Frank.

"I ain't seen him," Angie says first, words out before Hettie has wiped the hair from her face. The woman wears her usual, oddly shaped hat, the one that looks like a sailboat on her head. At least, it does in dry weather. Now, wet and furred with snow, it hangs down around Hettie's face, bobbing forlornly as she edges into the bar.

Angie has never served the woman, never raised a glass in her direction and, as Hettie moves slowly into the room, Angie sees again how much Hettie hates the place. The woman places her feet carefully, as though on ice. She wears leather boots that disappear under her skirts.

"You haven't seen him at all?" and her voice is hoarse and rough. She lives with her son on the edge of town and Angie wonders how Hettie can care for him.

The boy is disabled, Angie knows, though she has heard Hettie describe it bluntly. When Hettie once came looking for Frank, she said her boy was an imbecile. It was an odd, shocking word that Angie hated.

"Someone said he'd be here," Hettie persists. A tick flutters in her eyelid, so to Angie, for an odd moment, it looks as though she is winking.

"Which someone? I tell you, he ain't been in. Not seen him for days." This is true, though Angie's dander is up and she knows her response is automatic – she would have lied to Hettie any-way, for shits and giggles. Hettie gets under her *skin*.

"Jackie told me." Hettie glares around the room, as though her man might spring out from the wood panelling.

"Jackie ain't been in here, either." Again, true, at least for the week since Ray Sullivan's party. But Angie says it to make a point and says it louder than necessary.

Hettie finally seems to get it. She gives a sigh and heaves herself back to the door. The hem of her long skirt is dripping wet and smears the floor, though she doesn't notice. What she feels, instead, is cold and, beneath that, the white flint of rage.

Hettie leaves Shay's Bar and Angie and Gerry in it, the two staring absently at each other. Frank is not there; Hettie hadn't really believed she would find him so easily, but Jackie seemed so sure. The miner had leaned against the wall of the store and nodded his head: "Oh, yes, I seen Frank in the bar, just as I was passing. He'll be there now, I reckon."

And Hettie had taken the odd, sweetly spoken man at his word.

Now she feels a fool. She has tramped all the way across town upon hearing the news, abandoning thoughts of buying yesterday's stale bread from the storeman - and Frank isn't even in the bar.

She stands in the battering wind outside Shay's, flakes licking at her coat, cold settling into the damp creases of her skin. Frank, truth be told, could be anywhere, and she knows the odds are against finding him. He leads me a merry dance, she thinks, longing and hatred trampling her chest like attacking birds.

So she does the only thing she can do, and that is to turn tail and tramp back home, past the store and the mine and the chapel, alongside the stream that runs on the outskirts of Stokeland whatever the temperature. She has yet to see it freeze over and home is about a mile along the water's trail.

And Hettie hurries. Ernest is not good when left with strangers and, even though he knows Mrs Naylor, their neighbour, he can still act up. Hettie pounds her boots into the snow, urging her bones on, back to her son. She is hungry: the smell of chilli at Shay's Bar, though unfamiliar, made her mouth sting. But she had not the means to pay for it. Frank hasn't left her money in an age; whenever she wants to speak to him about it, the man is nowhere to be found.

"But he comes to see *me*," Ernest tells her from time to time, cheerful, even though all she can give him for dinner is day-old porridge thickened with sawdust. Hettie remembers her daddy stirring a bowl of the same, in Ireland, when the potatoes went bad and they had to kill their chickens, before they gave up and took a boat to America. She hopes she gave her father the same pleased, unquestioning smile that Ernest gives her when he eats. A smile that says he is hungry and he trusts her to provide.

The honesty shines from Ernest's face when he says he has been visited by his father, but Hettie has yet to see him. And, even though she does not mean to, she gets angry with her son when he talks about Frank. "You should tell me when he gets here – he shouldn't be sneaking into your room like a criminal," and Ernest's face would fall, and Hettie would feel wretched. It isn't the boy's fault – she sincerely believes that his father is to blame for their poverty.

She trudges home, thinking these things, anger filling her belly where food does not. She had fallen in love with Frank's tales and fancies, but stories about mystical lands and cities in the sky fed no one in the snow.

Ernest sees her before Mrs Naylor and is up, up out of his chair and out of the door, thin arms around her waist. Hettie looks down at him, pleased, but feels an ache as she takes in her son's white face, hunger hollowing out his cheeks. It is as though his skin is emptying, she thinks, shedding the fat and ripples that children have – *should* have – so that Ernest seems...oh, not real, somehow.

And yet he is real enough to her, and he is patting down her pockets, searching for bread. Mrs Naylor has fed him – Hettie sees a bowl of stew over the boy's shoulder – and the fact he has eaten some is testament to his hunger. Hettie struggles to get Ernest to eat anything other than porridge, bread and a paste she found in the store, one made from nuts. She hasn't got that today: her pockets hold nothing.

Ernest is making a noise, a cowl, and she drops to her knees so their noses touch. Mrs Naylor narrows her eyes from her seat at the table but Hettie ignores her. She knows her son better than anyone, has calmed him this way since birth. She puts her hands on either side of his face and pulls him close, feeling his sweet breath slowing.

"We'll eat tonight," she says quietly and swallows Ernest's mewling disappointment.

"There's food on the table," Mrs Naylor interjects, and makes a show of rattling the bowls. "*Proper* food. Milk loaf and peanut butter won't make a boy grow."

"Thank you, Mrs Naylor," and Hettie stands, pulling her son against her. "We'll be going now. Ernest, say goodbye to Mrs Naylor."

Ernest mumbles and wriggles inside his woollen jumper. He has resisted Mrs Naylor's attempts to dress him in a tracksuit, which had belonged to her son. He refused, shying away from the curious, shiny fabric, but not before touching it.

Hettie takes her son back out into the snow and they walk the short distance across a white field towards their house. It is a rough block of wood, a room at the bottom and two above, a window on each floor. Rags are packed around the seams of the building in a futile attempt to keep in the heat. Hettie swings open the door and they enter, and she turns to wad the gap between door and earth with a piece of carpet she found at the town dump. Ice is smeared on the inside of the hut's window and the stove has gone out.

She takes off her sodden hat and sits Ernest down on the one armchair. Bends in front of the stove, numb fingers fighting to light the kindling. After several attempts she manages, and a mean strip of flame struggles for life. She turns to scoop Ernest up, heart thumping wetly as she notes how light he is, and they hug, the boy fitting into the curve of her side.

A basket of sewing sits by the chair and, once Ernest is asleep, Hettie reaches round and scoops up a ball of mending, though it takes a while to thread the needle with her frozen fingers. She takes what mending she can from around the town and today the basket holds socks. Some of the items shock her, with their bright, garish colours; she wonders how the wool was dyed in that way. The patterns, too – swirls, animals, phrases. She can't see how the weaver did it, creating such things.

In the dim light Hettie sews. She mends holes, pulling together threads and seaming gaps and tears together with tiny, practiced stitching. She is known as someone who mends well, who can repair where others might have given up. Clothes are precious, here in Stokeland, with the town's intermittent deliveries. She has found enough work, over the years, to keep her and her son going – just about. As Ernest snores beside her, their bodies melded together, Hettie turns the fabric over in her icy fingers, not noticing the sharp prick of the needle.

She remembers how, in the early days with Frank, just a few months after landing in New York, she sewed his clothes. She remembers washing and cutting up an old rag, dragging colour back into the garment. It pains her, now, to think of it; how she started subtly, lining Frank's trouser pockets with a purple square, so that only he would see when he pulled out his coins. She winces to think of how she added red panels to the inside of his coat, padding it out for winter but, she hoped, letting him know in a silent way that she could *do* for him – that he would find her a good enough wife. When they married, her father refusing to give his blessing, Hettie made her own skirt; thick waistband, green panel almost up to her bust, the kind she had seen the ladies wear back in Ireland before they abandoned their land.

Frank never seemed to see her work, though; never seemed to see her bent over a ball of fabric against the light of the fire. Instead he carried on with his stories, practising them out-loud so he'd be ready to entertain those in the bars and saloons of Brooklyn.

Ernest snorts and farts, a sour smell wrinkling Hettie's nose. The oats and bread he eats fill his stomach with air. She wonders what his guts will be like, later, after Mrs Naylor's broth. And, again, she thinks how hungry he must have been to eat it.

She remembers that Frank eats anything. Week-old fish, seal, even horse. She senses there was little food in his childhood but never asked. He is Irish, too, but debt, rather than the blight, sent him across the water, to New York where he became known as the Story Man. She first saw him standing on a corner, near to the market stalls, holding sway with his wild tales and legends. The Irish around him loved it, loved the way his word-pictures transported them home to peat and broth and family. For the first time in her life, Hettie had been foolish and they married quickly. But there was no money to pay for a doctor when the time came, and she woke to find herself on a cart being wheeled from the city, a new baby tucked in beside her. She wondered if she was lucky to be alive, but Frank, the man who could weave tales from the air, barely spoke of those three days she couldn't remember.

Her own stomach growls. She swallows drily. The memory of the spiced meat from Shay's Bar; Stokeland has flavours and tastes that overwhelm her. Sometimes she picks up packets in the store, turning the bright colours in her fingers. She can't understand what they contain and the shouty, garish words on the front make her nervous. So Hettie buys bread, dried eggs, oats, the paste Ernest likes, and what little meat she can afford.

She can't remember when they arrived at Stokeland, or even if Frank was with them. Ernest had grown a little, Hettie is sure, so they'd lived in the snow for a least a few years. She reaches the end of her mending, thinking back to what Frank had said, how he had persuaded them to come here. A town, north – far north – which had men to entertain with stories, and food, lots of food. It did not take the battering wind and the fall of snow long to hammer home that it was a lie. That it was another of Frank's fanciful tales and that the city in the clouds was just that. Air.

A figure passes the window and Hettie looks up. Night comes early to Stokeland, but the gloom is not so thick that she cannot make out a man's shape, wrapped up against the cold. Short, stout, bowed legs poking beneath a heavy coat. She can see it is Connor, the fella who is never far from Jackie's side. Hettie watches Connor make his lumbering way past. She sees how his legs barely hold him and how they buckle outwards, in a way that makes her wince. She wonders how he manages working down the zinc mines, and if Jackie does the lion's share of the work. She knows they live in town, sharing a couple of rooms above the carpenter's.

Hettie is angry. Connor, she thinks, is making his way home, where Jackie will appear at some point. The same Jackie who lied to her, who told her Frank was in Shay's Bar when he wasn't. She wonders if Connor will start dinner and if Jackie will pick up meat from the store. She can see the kind of friendship they have. There were men, back in Ireland, who had similar friendships. It is not completely shocking to her, though Hettie's father used to steer his daughter into the nearest shop if their paths crossed, in town, with those kind of men.

Unlike her father, Hettie is not angry that these friendships exist. Instead, she is angry because Frank is nowhere to be seen and she is hungry and Jackie told her a lie.

So she gets up. It disturbs Ernest, who wakes and calls out, but that cannot be helped. She swings open the door to their shack, knowing the meagre, damp heat emitted by their stove will soon dissipate in the frigid air. But she doesn't care and steps out onto the snow.

"Connor!"

She wonders if he will hear her, for the wind is blowing now and it seems to pillow her shout back to her in a damp wave. But the bowed man does hear and turns. She sees his wide jaw and long mouth, and thinks that he looks like a toad, or what she remembers of toads back in Ireland.

Ernest has sidled out of the house as well, and stands in his socks. Hettie resists the urge to bark at him and tell him to go back inside.

"Hettie?" Connor squints in the darkening light and plods back across the snow-bound field. "Are you all right?"

Hettie clenches her fists, quickly, hiding them inside her sleeves. "Going home, Connor?"

"I am, yes. I was down that mine at four this morning. I've finished for the day."

"And will Jackie be waiting for you?"

Connor's step slows. He is shorter than Hettie and he looks up at her. He tilts his head. Curious. "Not yet, I imagine. But soon." He brings his square hands around to his middle and Hettie sees his thumbs press against each other, making an anxious kind of steeple.

Ernest folds himself against his mother's side and she feels a tremble pass through his body. He's cold, she thinks, and wraps an arm around him.

"Tell Jackie," and Hettie swallows, "that I don't like his games. He told me an untruth, and it was not kind."

Connor's eyes shoot up, an inverted reflection of his mouth, which has turned down. "I don't understand, Hettie."

"Just tell him that." Her voice is shriller than she'd like and Ernest sighs.

"Well. All right." Connor hesitates and makes to turn away. The dark spreads out, ready to swallow the man whole, and fill in the space Connor leaves like blood flooding into a wound. But then he swings back and Hettie sees how cruelly his legs move; how his knees twist almost back on themselves. It makes her bowels feel loose and hot, just to see. He speaks again. "Hettie, I don't know what Jackie said, but he isn't an untruthful man. I know him, better than anyone. He's the type to speak the truth even when he would do well to hold his tongue."

Hettie clenches her fists again, *squeeze squeeze*. "He said he'd seen Frank. Said he was in Shay's Bar, but he wasn't. Angie, that slattern who pulls the beer – she couldn't wait to tell me Frank was nowhere to be seen."

Connor tilts his head and his brown, almost amber eyes open and settle. He is thinking hard. Hettie can see that connections are being made in his mind, that understanding is weaving itself together like the pattern on a rug. "Jackie made a mistake, then. But it is true that Frank is in Shay's, most nights. Telling his stories."

"Maybe I'll come and see him," Hettie says suddenly. "Maybe I'll bring his child along with me and interrupt his tall tales. Let those who crowd around him hear how he explains away what it is like for a child to be little and hungry." She pulls Ernest's sleeve, trying to swing the boy from her side and in front, between her and Connor.

Ernest resists. He makes a small noise and

twists handfuls of his mother's skirt up beside his ears. Then his head pokes out, rabbit-like. "I saw him last night, Ma."

Connor looks down at the boy. He is not much taller than the child and can see how fragile Ernest's bones are, how his jaw is not rounded with smooth plump, like a child's should be. The boy's face is too wide and his eyes are out of focus. And yet Connor sees something else in the boy. A glint in Ernest, like a light in the distance.

The way Hettie clicks her tongue makes it clear that she does not see this light, in spite of the savagery of her love. She feels angry and thinks her boy is growing up to be like his father; full of stories. "And how did you manage that, Ernest? Did you walk all the way into town? Stand at the bar and drink ale while waiting for your father to finish with his horse-shit?"

It is a hard word and Connor sees the line of steel through Hettie; a line, no doubt, she has re-lied upon during her years in the Stokeland wilderness. He wonders if Frank has shaped her, whether in those first hot moments of love, or the empty years after.

Ernest, though, seems to glide under his mother's anger. He becomes languid, and relaxes his hold of his mother's dress. Dreamily, he says, "but I saw him. He came into my room and sat on the end of my bed. He told me about Quilaq."

Hettie shakes her head, snorting. He's so hungry he's lost all sense, she thinks.

She turns to Connor, eyes blazing, mouth open, ready to shout – and, suddenly, Connor wants to be away. He wants to leave this furious woman and make his way back to the rooms above the carpenter's store, where it is calm and peaceful. In those rooms, a bed stands behind a curtain and there is a couch, surrounded by books. They pile up like a fortress. He and Jackie read them all, ankles locking together in the evening as they sprawl.

Connor aches to be there now, and he nods swiftly, cutting Hettie off just as more words spill from her mouth. He turns and stumbles into the black, lumbering across the field towards home. He leaves her to shout into the air, to stand with her strange son and his strange memories.

Jackie isn't home and Connor is twisted up inside, though he can't quite work out why. It's a rippling, rendering feel in his stomach, and it makes him think of Shawnee, Oklahoma, when the dust came and, also, men with pitchforks.

Years ago, it happened – he isn't sure exactly when, just as he can't remember when they first came north, but Connor remembers Shawnee all right. Jackie had seen the posse first, through a crack in the barn where they'd taken shelter. A fist of men, swollen with hunger and no work, and keen to put their fury somewhere – they marched towards the barn. Jackie yelled they were coming and they should be ready to scarper. And, even though he shouted, Jackie hadn't sounded surprised; famine and ruined farms made targets of men like he and Connor.

There'd been similar incidents in Lincoln County. Occasionally the moment overtook them, and Connor and Jackie were not as discreet as they could have been. In Shawnee, someone had seen them in a bar – not even doing anything, but sitting together in a way that other men didn't. Later that night, they'd just about made it out of the barn before the door was beaten down - Jackie had run, tugging Connor and his sideways gait along with him. All the while, as his feet pounded, Connor felt his belly shake with fear. It was a feeling he had never been able to forget, despite the miles they put between them.

And the feeling in his stomach is back now, even though they are far away from dust and

Shawnee, Oklahoma. Connor leans against the window of their little room above the carpenter's, looking out over the snow flattening Stokeland, and tries to calm himself. But he cannot forget the dust clouds. He cannot forget the grit that seeped through clothes and burrowed into the corners of eyes. At night, if ever he had the privacy to undress – and a quiet space in a bunkhouse was as rare as a job itself - Connor used to find sand in his underwear. It got everywhere, causing his feet to rub painfully in boots too large for him, drying up his throat so it felt like days before he could swallow properly. After Jackie had taught him to read, he read about a man who fell asleep on his porch in Broken Arrow with his mouth open, and suffocated to death in a sudden gale. For a long time after, even when they made it to Stokeland, Connor carried a fear of sleeping outside.

He watches the dark settle on fields around the town and his legs sing. Twelve hours is a long time to squat down a zinc mine, even for Connor who was shaped for the work after his father helpfully broke his legs as a child. He wishes Jackie was around to see to him. Jackie always seemed to have a knack of working out the knots and lumps that appeared in the flesh around

Connor's knees; he knows how to rub them away and relax his friend's body.

He isn't sure where Jackie is. He should have been down the mine still, by rights, but, if Hettie is to be believed, he'd been at the store. Connor thinks of Hettie. How angry she was, shaking in her long dress. And how that strange child, Ernest, clung to her. Her love for the boy made her fierce - that Connor could see - and, though her coarseness frightened him (for she is, after all, a tall woman and he is a broken, small man), it is a coarseness he can understand. He understands that such anger comes from love, the kind that makes you crazy.

He stopped by the slaughterhouse on the tramp home and bought an off-cut of beef. Or horse, who knows? Connor takes it from his coat pocket and lays it on the table. Not much red meat, mostly gristle. The flesh is threaded with white fat running through the piece. He will have to boil it for a few hours to soften it up. There might be an onion somewhere, and maybe a beer or two. He shrugs off his coat and thinks about preparing the meal, trying to calm his churning stomach. He loves Jackie so much – the idea of him being with another man makes his skin blush with sorrow.

He pulls out a pan from a cupboard, each

motion a blur of pain. This pan – was Jackie thinking about Frank when he put it away? He steps over the piles of books fortressing the sofa. Does Jackie read to Frank, the way he does to Connor? Connor cannot see for a second and steadies himself against the table. Jackie has a voice like honey. The long drawl, the slow roll of words over his tongue. Connor closes his eyes and remembers the stories Jackie read to him, how the man devoured books. Even before Roosevelt's New Deal and the planting of all those trees to stop dust clouds gathering again, when there wasn't food to be found in the huddle of a storm, Jackie had a tattered copy of Jack London and read passages aloud to Connor.

Now, Connor hacks at an onion and thinks what he might do, if he were to meet Frank right now - right *now* - when he has a knife in his hand. The fella might have been at Ray Sullivan's party, the one he threw to celebrate divorcing Wanda, though Connor can't quite remember. Truth was, Connor had drunken too much himself that night. He'd not wanted to go – the thought of throwing a party to celebrate a love now gone saddened him. He'd made a point of avoiding Ray and stayed in the background when the man grew leery and smashed a glass. Paul Shay was a big man and he'd seen how Ray quaked when the bar owner demanded Ray *calm the fuck down.*

He can't remember if Jackie stayed beside him all night in the bar, either. They left together, for sure – Connor woke with Jackie's arm thrown over his thigh in the tangle of their bed.

But though he hasn't seen Frank for days, Connor remembers the power of the man's stories. He has been mesmerised like others in Shay's Bar, by the tales the man tells; of dragons and little men from Ireland, and women with long red hair and dresses up to their thighs. Frank has a honeyed tongue, too, just like Jackie, and spins his stories of other worlds and other lands as easily as silk. Men become caught up in them, twisted by the lilt and sway of the magic man.

The frying onion stings his eyes and Connor brings a shaking hand to his face. He imagines a drawing together of the storyteller and his lover. On the inside of his eyelids he sees how Jackie would be desperate to hear all about a land in the clouds. How it might be just the thing that would make him lie to Hettie.

❄

Jackie comes home. Connor hears him before seeing him, the man's heavy feet clumping off snow on the stoop of the carpenter's workshop. Their rooms are above where the carpenter conducts his business; sometimes they hear the whirl of the sander or the crack of splintering timber. They don't mind the smell of hot wood, pungent as leather, seeping into their home. On rest days from the mine, Connor likes to lie in bed and listen to the industry occurring, invisibly, on the floor below. He imagines curls of sanded wood, gathering like hair, billowing aside when a fellow barges in with a job for the carpenter. These imagined curls, they seem to remind him of a brother, a baby, whom he had forgotten.

Now, Jackie opens a door at the rear of the workshop and strides up. He sniffs as he enters their rooms, a theatrical motion that makes Connor's heart swing precariously in his chest - Jackie makes such a show of breathing in the scent of cooking meat, Connor knows, because he is pinched by guilt. Jackie cannot lie, is no good at it. He's never been able to bite down and swallow his words, or let them spill out in ways that conceal the truth. Making such a show over nothing-special-beef, boiling on their one-ringed stove and giving off an earthy aroma, makes Connor feels ashamed for his man.

He watches now, from his perch on the sofa, as Jackie wades into the room, looking like a man weighed down by his bones, and pulls off his boots. Connor stays curled under a blanket, book in hand, not reading.

"That smells fine, Con," Jackie says eventually, when the silence becomes too thick to ignore.

Connor nods.

Then, restlessness pooling under his skin, Jackie strides over to their bed. He pulls aside the curtain and changes his shirt. In the reflection of the window opposite the couch, Connor sees him: bare-chested, scars down his left side, running from his armpit into his pants. Jackie had a rough father, too. There are more on his back, from a belt buckle. They'd been enough to make even Connor – with legs bowed like a barrel – clench his fists and feel hateful when he saw them for the first time.

Some scars, though, that Jackie carries, are only a few years old. They'd been won, Jackie told Connor in the early days, when he'd misjudged a man or said something when it would be better to be quiet.

Jackie cannot bear quiet. That time when the mob at Gillymore broke his jaw and left him for Connor to find – it was the silence he had to keep as his bones knitted back together that hurt more than fists. He'd been lucky to be found in time, so the doc said, for his blood had gathered, treacherously, in his throat and lungs, and he might have drowned. "On land? We're thousands of miles from the ocean," Connor had spluttered, not understanding, and Jackie, too wounded and jaw wired shut, shook his head sadly. Later, when they holed up in Laker's Park and slept under the stars, Jackie could not even read – reading should be sociable, he'd told Connor early on. Reading should be done *out-loud.*

Connor remembers these things in the time it takes Jackie to change his shirt and sigh his way back to the sofa. Jackie sits down and, silence deepening, answers the unasked question. "Yes, I was with Frank."

Connor closes his eyes briefly. Jackie isn't like anyone he's ever met. He thinks back to where they first met, on a farm in Oklahoma, hauling a waggon of manure across a field. Connor could not reach the top of the load, not with his legs, but the farmer took him on anyway, mainly on account of his upper body strength. Connor could lock his forearms around a steer and never let go – a handy trick at branding time. Even now, Connor feels pride in the power of his arms. He swings a pick at Stokeland's mine with the best of them.

He'd worked the farm for a season before Jackie showed up, that day on the field. Wiry, sporting a fresh black eye, voice like slow-moving water. Connor couldn't stop looking at him.

"Bar fight," Jackie had said. Later he let Connor hold a wet rag against his swollen eyebrow while the others disappeared for chow time. And that had been that. Jackie had caught his hand and pulled him close, and Connor remembered a tumbling sensation. A swooning in his stomach and a certainty that those odd, secret feelings he'd had ever since being a boy – "that *sinful* thing of yours," one of his father's girlfriends had once hissed – would never be squashed down again. Not with Jackie around.

"I saw Hettie," Connor says, eventually. He has to blink away the memories and the yearning to reach out to touch his man almost overpowers him. He remembers he is angry. "She said you'd told her Frank was at Shay's Bar."

"I did." Jackie bows his head. "A lie. Yes, it was. I am ashamed."

"But why? Why lie to her? What were you doing with Frank?" Connor holds himself still. Images of Jackie and Frank together hurt his throat and he swallows hard.

Jackie rubs his palms, the sound dry and slippery. Outside it is dark. A bird makes a wracking shout and they hear the turn and settle of snow. Connor waits, knowing Jackie will answer.

He does. "Do you remember that time in Gillymore, when they broke my face?"

"I do."

"Kicked one of them in the guts first, did I tell you? He squealed like a piglet." Jackie smiles at the memory. "You found me. All busted up and flat on my back."

"I thought you were dead."

"Yes. Well, you found me. We dug out that hole in Laker's Park and stayed there for a few weeks while I healed."

Connor nodded and waited, again.

"I was going crazy, wasn't I, not able to read to you? Jaw shattered to pieces, unable to talk."

The stew on the stove pops and Connor wonders if it has burnt. He doesn't get up.

"I told Frank about it at Ray Sullivan's party. Don't know why. Just seemed to spill out. And he told me it happened to him once. Owed money and a couple of men beat him up. We were just talking."

"And tonight?"

"I quit the mine early today. Not sure why.

Just needed to find him. He *was* on the way to Shay's but he stopped."

"And?"

"We *talked*, Connor, is all. He has this..." Jackie waves his land, coiled fingers wrapping around air. "He told me about this place he's heard of. Somewhere people like us can be safe."

"Quilaq?" Connor thinks of Ernest and the angry way Hettie turns on him. "It's a story, Jack. Kind of thing you tell kids."

"You've heard of it?" Jackie's eyes are wide.

Connor shrugs. "It's a fairy-tale. And, besides, we *are* safe here. Here we can eat, work. Love."

Jackie is silent again and suddenly Connor feels panic. He wonders what kind of place Jackie is seeking – if it's somewhere without him. Somewhere where Connor is not.

The snow comes, the snow comes, and when Connor follows Jackie out of their little apartment and down the steps to the world outside, he is struck by how smooth and white and clean the earth appears. The carpenter's rubbish pile, usually a mass of splintered timber or broken pieces of furniture beyond rescue, has been rounded by millions of tiny white flakes, and is no longer a jagged mash of weapons. Connor stares at the mound, thinking of the many times he has been comforted by the presence of sharp wooden daggers, taking heart in such ready access to weapons should men with pitchforks come. Seeing the rubbish pile so transformed and now so innocuous shames him. It is just a gathering of wood, after all, made innocent by snow. And, look, the latrine! such a foul-smelling, dirty wooden shack – it has been transfigured into an inviting grotto. The putrid smell carries on the air, though, and makes Connor's nostrils flare.

Jackie's boots leave heavy footprints in the snow, white smears going up his calves. It is so deep Connor thinks Jackie's boots will come off and be inexorably, unavoidably sucked into the powder. But whilst Jackie has to pull and make a deliberate effort to move, his body jerking like a lazy toddler being forced to walk, his boots stay on and he makes slow, steady progress towards the road.

They are going to find Frank. Jackie had suggested it, his voice barely above a whisper. "I have a mind he's be at Paul Shay's," he'd said. "Just come and listen to him."

"He's a storyteller," Connor had said, redundantly. "It's how he makes a living, whatever kind of living it is. Not that he gives anything to Hettie or his son."

"That's none of our business," and Jackie had got up, reached for his coat and thrown Connor's to him. "Just hear what he's got to say. I promise it will be worth it."

"What kind of thing will he tell me?" Connor asked, watching himself put on his coat, amazed at the treachery of his body. He did not want to go out again. He wanted to stay where it was warm, eat the stew he'd cooked and, eventually, find a way to forgive Jackie. It was how it went – how it had always been. Before they got to Stokeland, Jackie would sometimes take off, maybe for as long as a week. He'd just disappear and, when he'd return, he'd be different. The way he moved, the way he stood with a tilt to his hips – Connor knew he'd been with other men. But Connor always found a way to forgive him. It was how it was.

But now, trudging after Jackie in the snow, Connor feels frightened. This seems different. There is an urgency, a mobility to Jackie that he is not used to. In the past, when there were other men, Jackie returned home with a languorous kind of air. An indolent ease that rippled out in the way he spoke and moved. As though he were sated.

Connor is not used to seeing such energy in his man after Jackie had been with someone else and, somehow, it gladdens his heart and lifts his spirits. Maybe all Jackie *really* did with Frank was talk, Connor thinks. He senses Jackie would be different if some other kind of transaction had occurred. With that in mind, Connor tries to move his bowed legs faster and catch up with the fellow.

"Hulloo!" A cry from behind them and Connor turns, awkwardly, joints protesting. It is already too cold for him. He squints into the falling snow and makes out two figures, shadows, gliding towards him. For a mad second he feels panic and remembers that terrifying book Jackie read to him last winter – *Dracula*. They'd lain their coats on top of their blankets and huddled deep into their bed while Jackie read, black tongues licking the walls as their one candle burned. The book had been too good to leave until the morning so Jackie had bought a bundle of candles at the store and stayed up late, reading out-loud. Connor sees the Count now, moving but not moving, making his terrible way towards him, over the snow, not leaving a trail.

He cries out, a yelp, and Jackie turns back, with an exasperated "what is it, man?"

And it is only Hettie and Ernest. Hettie is

wearing her long coat, the one that falls to her feet, and Ernest is wrapped up in blankets. As they near, Connor sees Hettie has tied rope around Ernest's middle, securing the blankets in place but producing the effect of turning the boy into a trussed-up piece of meat. Like a pork joint, Connor thinks, and feels sad for the poor, coatless child. But Ernest seems happy enough – he beams when he spots Connor.

"We're going to see Dad!" he says brightly. His bare little ears are red and sore with cold. Connor takes off his own hat and forces it down on the boy's head.

Hettie approaches. She stares at Jackie, anger still raw and blazing. Snowflakes stick to her clothes and melt quickly, the heat of her body obviously too much.

"You lied to me, Jackie." Hettie's eyes are wet and bruised, and set too far back in her head.

Jackie looks down, to where his boots are hidden in the mounds of white. "I did. I'm sorry."

"Why did you? What did I ever do to you?"

"Nothing, Hettie. You're – you're a fine woman."

Jackie has no idea how to talk to women and the words he mutters are, Connor knows, from a book. Yet they seem to have some effect on Hettie, for her shoulders settle and her head bounces forward on her neck, deflated. "I just want to know where he is, Jackie. I can't remember the last time I saw him."

"I saw him last night!" Ernest said, joyfully and simply. He looks around him, at the settling and rising earth, wonder on his face. "The houses are disappearing!"

It is not true, of course; it's just the snow coming down harder than ever, but Connor looks about him with a jump. He has never seen snow like this in Stokeland and realises that, if they don't move quickly, they'll never make it to Shay's Bar.

"We should go, Jackie," he says, nudging the fellow. "Shay's will be covered before we know it."

"You're going to Shay's Bar?" Hettie's eyes harden.

"We are. I think, I think maybe Frank will be there. Really, this time." Jackie offers up a small smile.

"Where was he before? You knew, didn't you? Why did you lie?"

Jackie breathes in deeply and, when he exhales, the cloud rises upwards, a film of lace stretching above them. "Come with us. To Shay's. Frank knows about a place. Where he was earlier – when I said he was at the bar – he went to fetch things. He has maps. Directions."

"Quilaq!" Ernest shouts.

It takes them much longer than they all expect, but the snow comes down relentlessly and plays cruel tricks on their feet; a step forward becomes a step sideways, a lurch ahead becomes a staggering fall. More than once, Hettie is helped to her feet by Jackie. Connor holds Ernest's hand and tugs him on. The man's gloves are on the boy's hands, Connor's now frozen fingers screaming his hatred for Frank, a father who couldn't make sure his son was properly dressed in the frigid north. The group blunder on, towards town and Shay's Bar.

"This is a fool's mission," Hettie says through clamped teeth, as Jackie props her up again and they struggle alongside a fence. "We should be indoors on a night like this. Is it worth dying out here in the cold to go and listen to one of Frank's stories?"

"It ain't a story, Hettie," Jackie says, his voice cottony in the falling snow. "I've heard of the place. You must have, surely."

If Hettie can shrug, she shrugs now, though

there is too much white stuff on her shoulders to make the gesture worthwhile. Inside she rues that fact – she has always been an *emphatic* shrugger. "Children's stories. Nothing more than fancies you tell babies at night."

"I don't think so. Gerry the Gin – he told me one night that he's seen the place. Shadows, anyhow. And smelt it."

"Codswallop!" Hettie laughs angrily. "Gerry the Gin doesn't get his name for nothing, Jackie. There are so many of his kind in this town."

"Gerry's a good man."

Hettie sniffs dryly. "Well, you may know better than I. But I've seen the men round here. They work and booze all the time God sends, just so they can earn enough to head south, to Tramper's Creek. But none of them leave. None of them make it out of here. Instead they sit their hours at Shay's Bar, lining that greasy bastard's pockets."

Jackie's mouth falls open in a soft "o"; Hettie's rage has made her coarse. He can see that anyone might stray into the firing line and be seared by her hot tongue. But he wants to speak. Has to speak.

"People do leave, Hettie. Ray Sullivan – he trades at Tramper's Creek. He doesn't spend all his time drinking. I think your heart is harder than it needs to be."

Behind them, Ernest falls over again and laughs. Jackie sees Connor haul the boy to his feet and shake his head. Jackie's man is incredulous that the boy can't see that they're in a bit of a fix. Anxiety is catching; as the snow thickens and crusts about them, Jackie urges his feet on. He doesn't fancy a night out in the stuff.

"Ray had a fine time in Tramper's Creek, didn't he?" Hettie says. Her mouth is a curled smirk. "So much so that Wanda divorced him."

Jackie says nothing to this, but wonders where Hettie hears her news. She doesn't come into Shay's, only when on the prowl for Frank.

"What has he told you about this place that's so special?" Hettie asks after a time. The moon is out and blazing, sallow light reflecting in the diamond dust piled along the trail. "Frank has lots of stories."

"I think everyone knows this place, really. If they try to remember hard enough, they'll know they've heard the name. *Quilaq*. Supposedly it's a town further north, way past the Kirk Straits. Only it's not on a normal map, not a map you can pick up at the store." Jackie grins into the wind, thinking of the storeman's yelps the time Jackie unfolded map after map – without paying for any of them. "The folk that live there must move, or something. Pack up camp every now and then."

"So a group of folk want to live out in the snow? What's special about that? We do, don't we – here in Stokeland?"

"I can't quite remember why I came here," Jackie says, screwing up his face. "I just seemed to make it here, is all. Something bad happened in Gillymore, where Connor and I lived. I was busted up, pretty bad. If you ask Connor he'll say he thought I was going to die." He glances again at his man, and at his thick arms. Arms that scooped Jackie up that day a gang tried to destroy his face. He'd carried Jackie away, and dug a hole in Laker's Park where they healed and hid. "After I got better, we came north. Must have heard about the mine and the work to be had. Why'd you come here?"

"Frank," Hettie says simply. "He brought us. I'd had a bad time with Ernest – the lying in, and all that." She dips her head down and Jackie can see she is embarrassed. "Childbirth is a nasty business, though I don't suppose you'd know about that. Frank says he thought the baby would die and then me. That's all he'll tell me. By the time I came round, we were on our way here. But I think Frank was trying to run away from someone, too."

She stumbles and Jackie reaches out, to prop her up. His arm is around her waist; he is struck by how slender she is. Her anger makes her big, but that seems to be melting a little. Her splintery ribs move beneath his fingertips. The ridges of her spine make him ache to hold her close, though the desire is one of comfort, not in the same way he aches at times for Connor. Hettie turns in Jackie's arms and allows herself to be held against him. The snow is white and canvassing, and she shines like a green jewel.

"I did listen to him, in the first days," she says softly. "Frank would come home and watch me nurse Ernest. We'd sit in that shack, with the snow coming in under the door, and he'd light the stove and watch. He cared a little, back then. Sometimes he'd disappear for days but he'd come back and say he'd been searching for some place, or talking to people who knew about it."

"What did Frank tell you?" Jackie asks. Warmth creeps between their bodies and their legs stride together.

Another flop from behind and Ernest is over again. Connor curses and Jackie hears a wet thwack as Ernest is pulled up and slung over the man's shoulders.

"He said that there was a town, or maybe a camp – maybe he said camp – where there always seemed to be *enough*."

"Enough food?" Jackie says and thinks of Gerry's story, about smelling baking and roasting, where the smell of baking and roasting had no business being.

Hettie's mouth folds at the side. She's thinking. Dimples appear in her cheeks – Jackie can see she was once a striking woman. "Not food, exactly. But yes, food, you could say. And other things. Enough warmth and firewood, which seems incredible out in the tundra. He said -" Hettie stops and gives a tired laugh.

"He said what?"

Hettie is shaking her head. "This is when I stopped listening to him. It was one of the times he held Ernest. There weren't many of them, mind. He doesn't like to touch his son and I don't think I'll ever understand it." Hettie looks over her shoulder at the boy, dangling across Connor's back, a dazed grin splitting his wide face. "Frank said he thought he was marking time before he found Quilaq. That here, where we live, is like a *holding* to him. That was Frank, always thinking about what isn't real."

❄

Gerry wakes up with a start, jerking his head upright so forcefully that he feels the bones in his neck grind together. He groans and reaches round to rub the muscles holding his puny head up, feeling whispery skin. *When did I become so old?* he thinks, fingers catching on cords of hair, hair that has not been cut for longer than he can remember and winds down his back. I used to laugh at men with hair like this, he thinks, remembering a tramp that wandered the village on Skye before the war, frightening the mothers.

His mouth tastes like curdled milk. An empty stub of whiskey sits at his elbow. His eyes feel bruised and a sour burp burns in his throat. Next to him is a woman. Her head is bowed over the bar, legs dangling precariously from a stool. Gerry blinks and looks around – ah, he is in Shay's Bar. It is dark outside and the bar is lit by just one lamp above the time-bell, an obsolete item that has never been used to clear the punters from the place. He reaches out, tentatively, to touch the woman's dyed blonde head – he cannot remember the last time he touched a woman's hair. Maybe it was his wife, the woman who was briefly his for a short, tender summer, before the baby and a narrow birth canal took her away. His heart aches in his chest. He wants to plunge his hands into the woman's hair, feel the slide of it under his fingernails. But the woman sits up abruptly, mirroring Gerry's jolt into consciousness only a few moments before. It is Angie. Her face has been creased by the edge of the bar; a pink fold lies on her skin like a knife mark. Gerry knows it is only sleep that has done this to her, but he cannot look at it – the sight of a scarred woman has always distressed him. He pulls his hands back to his side, ashamed.

Angie hasn't noticed his discomfort. She surveys the empty glasses. She laughs. "Wow. How much did we drink? If Paul walks in and sees this, he'll pitch a fit." She gets up, shaky-legged and, one hand on the bar at all times, edges her way behind the pumps and optics. Now she stands in her usual spot and Gerry feels the world right a little – that's where Angie should be, he thinks. Serving me drinks, not at my side getting as wasted as I. But, her hair...he closes his eyes and sees a farm and a gathering of sheep, and a yellow-haired woman with a rounded belly.

Angie makes a circle with her arms and scoops the glasses together into a huddle. Then grabbing handfuls of shot glasses, transfers then to the sink. "Why did we use so many?" she asks. "Why didn't we just rinse out a glass and refill it?"

Gerry comes back to himself, shaking away the memory of his wife. But he can't answer Angie – he has no idea why they drank the way they did, just as he has no idea who has paid for it all. Certainly not him. He remembers Angie giving him chilli and pushing him to talk about something – what was it? He's pretty sure that, whatever it was, his memory and his tongue was eased by Yukon Jack, and that Angie encouraged him to neck the whiskey as quickly as water.

"Angie," he starts. "I don't know what happened here – I've got a head that feels like it's going to burst – and I can't remember much. Only thing is, Angie, I..." he pats his pockets and drops his eyes. He is a poor man and has little, and sleeps outside in all weathers, but he has pride. It hurts him to say he has no money to pay for something he has quite obviously taken.

Angie waves him away and turns on the hot tap, swishing glasses around clumsily. "Looks as though we stuck to Yukon Jack, and my stomach feels as though I've had just as much as you. I'll tell Paul I dropped a bottle. Whenever he shows up."

"Paul will be out somewhere in the snow, looking for clouds that look like bears." A disembodied voice from some black place, in the thick of the darkened bar. Gerry feels the hairs on the backs of his hands stand up; the skin of his neck feels electric. It is not a voice he can immediately place – it hangs in the air like an orphan.

"Who said that?" Angie has no fear and squints into the bar. She makes a hurried movement and switches on a light, throwing the place into brightness. Gerry turns around, the shine from the bulb giving him courage.

It is man, tucked away in a booth. Frank. He is wearing his usual brown overcoat and it has flapped over on one knee. Gerry can see garish red lining that Frank once told him had been sewn by Hettie. Gerry knows a little of Hettie – he finds it hard to believe she would choose a colour so brazen.

"Paul will be out there in the snow," Frank repeats. He leans forward, elbows on the table. In the glare of the bar lights, his skin looks paler than ever. Yet his eyes...Gerry stares. Frank's eyes are round, just like sovereigns. They sit on his face as if drawn by a child. They is no shaping to the edges, just circles ringed by grey skin. They manage to simultaneously age and add youth to his face.

Gerry jerks, again, blinking furiously. Had he fallen asleep? His mind feels cloudy, as if he'd been hypnotised. He looks around, at Angie, wondering if the same thing is happening to her

– if Frank's curious gaze has put her in a trance, too. Gerry clears his throat – *listen to yourself, man. Too much whiskey and you start imagining.*

Angie is looking over towards Frank's booth, but not at him – instead, at the drink on the table. A tumbler full of honey-coloured water. Frank has helped himself, that much is apparent. Gerry can see Angie's face struggle for control. She is angry that the man has gone behind the bar to sort himself out, and frustrated that she cannot challenge him. Not with the whiskey stubs still in the sink and the smell of unpaid-for liquor in the air.

"I told Paul a story, once," and Frank stands up and drifts over to the bar. He brings his drink with him, holding it carefully in a flattened palm. Gerry has a strong urge to shrink back. Or to hop over the bar beside Angie.

"About animals who live in clouds," Frank continues. "Children's tale, nothing more. But since then, I've noticed he likes to stand and look at the sky." He closes and opens his eyes in that slow way of his – not blinking, exactly, for the motion seems too methodical. "How are you, Angie? Has the week been good to you?"

He settles himself down at the bar and tips the glass to his lips. "Seems as though you've had quite a drink, here. What could you have been talking about, to make you take to the booze in such a way?"

Angie doesn't answer Frank at first, but presses her hands, palm-first, down on the bar. Gerry can see her fight to reign in her indignation. Frank is drinking whiskey he hasn't paid for, and that isn't how it goes in Stokeland. Transactions are conducted; maybe not with money, but exchanges occur. A sack of coke for the fire is swapped for a crate of potatoes, a side of caribou for a set of good winter blankets. It is possible to lie with a woman, Gerry has heard, for a pair of boots.

Sometimes, Gerry knows, Frank has bought his drink in Shay's Bar with stories, his words as honey-flavoured as the booze. But such an understanding is with Paul Shay, not Angie, and Angie is looking at him as though she wants to bury her fingers in his strange, perfectly round eyes.

And, for no reason he can fathom, Gerry the Gin is suddenly very sure that such an act, such an outburst of fury on Angie's part would be calamitous. He can't understand it, but certainty pounds his temples, step for step with the whiskey-headache. Frank is important tonight. Frank is *very* important.

Gerry leans over and covers Angie's hands with his own. She looks down in surprise and he feels the flutter of her fingers as she tries to break free. But Gerry holds on and, over his shoulder, speaks to Frank.

"We were talking about Quilaq, Frank. Not very often I say the word out-loud, but there it is." Gerry feels Angie's hands become still and, feeling that she has also recognised the significance of Frank being here tonight, lets her go.

Frank has set his glass down on the bar and rested his chin on a criss-cross of fingers. He blinks in that way of his, once, twice.

And then it takes Gerry a while to realise Frank is talking. He thinks he hears music, at first; a rich loamy sound, sliding into the bar. Words tumble out and take shape, and Gerry shakes himself. Frank's mouth is moving.

"...in Hell's Kitchen. In a bar on 39th Street, the smell of the tannery mixing in with the beer. That's where I'd first heard of it. An old-timer, on the make just like me – he had them wrapped round his finger, so he did. Tramped to the Canadian North, he said, where he'd found Quilaq. I tried telling Hettie about it but...that woman. But why do you talk of Quilaq?"

Angie shifts behind the bar, transferring her weight lightly from one foot to the other. "I can't really remember how it came up, Frank. But Gerry and I – we both knew of the place. Somehow."

"Where is Quilaq, Frank?" Gerry asks. "Have you found it?"

Frank shakes his head. "Not I. I might have found a map that can take us there." He pats his breast pocket and there is a crinkling sound. "By God, I hope it does."

"What is it about this place?" From Angie. "Why do you want to find it, so?"

Gerry is aware that his body has tensed, skin feeling tight around his bones. He remembers mumbled conversations with the Inuit, the old chap he'd stumbled across on one of his hunting trips – the fellow had whimpered with gratitude beside Gerry's fire and talked through chattering teeth. He'd been on a hunt for a mysterious place in the snow, a town that was not really a town but not really a camp, either. A place so close the Inuit and his friends could smell the roasting of meat and the brazen, ripe smell of baking bread. A place called Quilaq, drawing the Inuit to it, though he had yet to find it. In Shay's bar, waiting for Frank to speak, Gerry is very aware he wants to know the answer to the question –

just what it is that pulls men to the invisible place.

"I think," Frank says, slowly, "that Quilaq is a place where no one ever goes hungry. Do you know what it's like to feel empty and know there's nothing to eat, that there won't be for days and days? When the potatoes rotted, my father killed our chickens. And then the cow. And then he pushed me into the bars to tell stories while my sisters ate grass."

"Where was this?" Angie asks, and Gerry sees she has softened a little.

"In Ireland. Hettie felt hunger, too." Frank circles his fingers round the glass and Gerry is surprised to see his eyes are wet. A faint tremble comes into Frank's voice. "I think anyone who finds Quilaq never has an empty belly. I want to find such a place and never leave."

Gerry understands and knows that hunger, having eaten only when successful with a snare. But, listening, he cannot help but feel a ripple of disappointment. Quilaq a place of abundant food? Is that all?

He sees the confusion in Angie's face, too. She is chewing the side of her mouth, her forehead a crease. "I'm not sure that's all there is to this place," she says.

"There's more, I'm sure. I talked to Jackie

about it – he has this *life*, you know," Frank says, looking at her. "Quilaq might be a place where he can live it, truly. With Connor or whoever. Where did you hear of it?"

"I can't remember," and Angie halters. Gerry can see she feels foolish. "It's a place I've always known about it, I think. I thought -" she gives a short, embarrassed laugh – "I thought of my grandmother when Gerry first said it. I have no idea why – the old bird died years ago. I am sorry for you, Frank, for knowing that kind of hunger. I haven't."

"The question is," Gerry says, clearing his throat, "where is it? I've walked the land for miles around Stokeland and never found it." He holds up his hand. "I'm not saying it's a story though, Frank. I think I was close enough, once, to smell cooking and mighty fine it was. I talked to Jackie about it, too."

"What about Ray?" Angie says, suddenly. She looks at the puzzled expression on Gerry's face and falters. "Ray Sullivan? He travels more than anyone I know, even more than you Gerry. Goes down to Tramper's Creek, at least once a month. Tries to sell the Inuits electrical appliances, he says, though what they would want with a sunbed beats me."

Frank's face screws up, as though, like Gerry, he cannot understand. Angie sighs.

"He's maybe heard something about where this place is. From the Inuits he talks to? If you have a map, he should take a look."

Frank's face clears and becomes serene once again. His voice becomes mellifluous. "Ray, then. We should talk to Ray."

"He was in here a week ago," Gerry says. "His divorce party."

Angie opens her mouth to speak when the door to the bar bangs open, and a wall of white powder sweeps into the room. There are figures amongst them: wet, black shapes shivering into Shay's. The door closes, is forced shut, and the screeching wind outside is muffled. The interlopers gather themselves, shake water from their shoulders, push back damp hair.

A boy's voice rings out. It is Ernest. "Dad!"

The atmosphere in the bar changes as snow-wet bodies step inside. Jackie reveals his face first, wiping away flakes that quickly turn to water in the heat of the place. His gloves feel sodden; he peels them off, gritting his teeth. They fall with a heavy slap to the floor.

He turns to Connor, who is gingerly pulling Ernest from his shoulder and standing the boy on the sticky carpet. Connor winces and Jackie knows his man is in pain – it has been a long walk. Instinctively he reaches out to touch him, to press down on Connor's screaming muscles and rub them, but he draws back. He remembers Gillymore and a hole in the ground at Laker's Park. Conditioned behaviour takes over and he offers a sympathetic smile instead.

Ernest is beaming down at the floor, at the wet circle pooling at his feet. He points and laughs – something about the patterns on the carpet amuses him – and looks up. He spies Frank and, making a babbling whoop of sound, shuffles over. The quilt that Hettie tied around him restricts the movement of his legs and he has to waddle, penguin-like. It only makes him laugh harder.

He nears Frank and, watching, Jackie is struck by the thought that this is the first time he has seen father and son together. In all the time he has lived in Stokeland – how long, now? – he has not witnessed Frank and Ernest in the same room, and now Jackie can do nothing but stare. Both have abnormally round eyes, though Ernest is skinny and underfed – his neck doesn't look strong enough to support a head with such cue-balls for eyes.

Something strange is occurring between them, standing a foot apart. Jackie feels a puckering in his stomach and arse, as though his body had been flooded with static. It ripples out from Frank and Ernest. Jackie hears a hum and imagines the air between man and boy becoming charged and white-hot. He glances at Connor, who is steadily stretching his body out but also watching Frank and Ernest closely.

"You feel it, too?" Jackie whispers.

"I do," Connor murmurs back. "Like the noise from the wireless when there's thunder in the air."

And then the moment passes, the static is gone, and Ernest has thrown his arms around Frank's waist. The man winces and Jackie remembers Hettie's words – that Frank did not like to touch his son. But, slowly, Frank drops his hand, slowly, stroking Ernest's hair.

Ernest chatters into Frank's coat. "I told Ma I'd seen you. She didn't believe me."

Frank leans over and Jackie hears him whisper. "Ah, but we have a special way of seeing each other, don't we Ernie?"

"Is that so?" and Hettie sweeps off her hat and shakes out her hair. The snow has melted her clothes to her and Jackie sees again what a fine woman she is. She has a shape that can make men weep. And the room crackles again, but not like before. This time, friction erupts between Hettie and Frank, in a way that everyone in the bar can sense and understand. Jackie cannot stop looking at Hettie's breasts, the fabric of her dress flat against them. He wonders, once more, almost for old time's sake, what it would be like to touch a woman.

Frank gently pushes the boy away from him and steps to the side, standing directly in front of his wife. He holds out his hands and, with a fearless motion, sweeps a finger along Hettie's cheek and down into the cup of her throat. Then, with a fluidity that makes someone in the bar gasp – Angie, Jackie thinks – Frank pulls the woman close and wraps his arms around her waist.

"She's going to murder him," Connor breathes, with certainty, and Jackie thinks he is right – he *must* be right, given the viper that spoke from Hettie's mouth the whole way over from her shack. She *hated* Frank for leaving her to raise their son alone, with no food and no money except for what she got for mending. The bitterness had exploded from Hettie like an ice-storm on their way over to Shay's Bar.

Except she does not kill him. Hettie does not

claw at Frank's face or knee him in the stomach. Instead she seems to...melt. Jackie flounders a little, to see it; he remembers a book he read a long time ago, though where he got it from he cannot say. A book about a meeting between two men, where nothing exactly seems to happen but a passing of looks, and somehow the men wake up in the same bed. Even now, standing in Shay's, Jackie can remember the fluttering he felt in his stomach as he read the words, and how, at fourteen, he knew with absolute certainty that he would be with a man.

"So, we're all here." Frank gleams around the room. Hettie is still pressed against him and she seems in no hurry to move away.

"All of us? What do you mean by that?" It's Gerry the Gin's voice. Jackie sees the old man sitting at the bar, close to Angie. Angie is wearing that garish floral shirt of hers that is un-buttoned far more than it needs to. Her skin is blotched and rough, but the way she looks at Gerry makes Jackie think something had hap-pened between them. He fights an urge to laugh. The absurdity of this night!

"What I mean, Gerry," Frank is saying, "is that we needed to be together this evening."

"Did we?" Connor.

"Can't you feel it?" Frank held out his hands,

palms up, as though balancing plates. And the hum, the static that they all registered when he met with Ernest, is back again, forceful this time. Jackie can hear it, like the distant rumble of a train. He feels a pull behind his belly-button and his feet move forward. He stands to the side of Frank and sees that Connor is moving, too. Gerry as well, and Angie stepping out from behind the bar.

Soon they have formed a circle, with Hettie and Ernest joining them. Frank stands in the middle. He looks at each of them in turn and touches his pocket. A crinkling sound. "We're going to set off on a journey, this night. And you, friends, know where we're going. We need each other to find it – I feel this is true. I feel it here." And he presses his hand to his stomach. "Maybe we need Ray as well, but maybe we'll find him along the way. And you know where we're going, don't you, friends?"

They do. Jackie squeezes Connor's hand and feels he has always known. Then, the group of them – Angie, Gerry the Gin, Jackie, Connor, Frank, Hettie and Ernest – speak as one. "Quilaq."

❄

Angie breaks the circle first, dropping Gerry the Gin's hand and turning away. Connor watches and sees the woman appears to be crying. He wonders why and then sees Jackie's face is wet, too. And Hettie's, and Gerry's. He lets go of Jackie's hand and touches his own cheeks, fingers sliding over damp skin, and he holds them in front of them, astonished. I didn't *feel* like crying, he thinks. His chest does not tighten the way it usually does when a good sob is on the way. And yet tears still slide from the corner of his eyes and trace a line into his hair. Connor's bewilderment doubles; why has his body begun to leak, so? And yet, as it does, he feels a kind of cleansing. He feels the dark marrow of occasional jealousy creep away, shards of mistrust edge away. He feels scooped out and empty, but in a deeply pleasurable way, as though his body is merely making room for light.

Perhaps the slopping of water has been caused by the strange, electric hum he can still hear. He can see no distress on the faces of those around him and yet they weep. Something is thrumming within them all.

Only Frank stays dry-eyed and he claps his hands together. "Let us find somewhere to sit. We have so much to plan."

Connor watches as the group do his bidding

and finds his own legs moving as well. He can't understand why his body is compelled to move at Frank's words. He doesn't know Frank as well as Jackie does. He has listened to the man's stories, sure, but only in company, in Shay's Bar, surrounded by whiskey-blurred men. He cannot say what it is about the man that makes his legs move to the sound of his voice. But they do and Connor takes a seat at the largest table in the bar.

Frank removes a folded sheet of paper from his coat pocket and lays it out on the table. It is a map. Connor hears Jackie click his tongue; his man brushes Connor's arm as he leans forward.

"Where did you find this map? Does it show Quilaq, Frank?" Jackie asks.

Frank shakes his head, smiling. "Now, wouldn't that make life beautiful? I woke up this morning and – I can't explain it – but this map was in my pocket. As if it had been there all the time and I never noticed. It doesn't show us where Quilaq is. But it does show something that will help us find it."

The group cranes forward.

Frank points at a place on the map. Angie squints down, wiping her eyes.

"I can't really see. Could I Xerox some copies for us all?"

Frank looks at her blankly, and Connor sees

Hettie and Jackie's brow crease as well. Ernest hoots.

"You make up words!" the child says. "What's that you're pointing to, Dad?"

"It's a stone man. The kind the Inuits build, though I don't know if they built this one." Frank looks round at them all. "It's huge, bigger than a sail boat."

Gerry the Gin clears his throat. "I've never come across it, Frank, and I've tramped and caught in these parts for more years than I can remember."

"And yet, here it is."

Angie makes another of her curious pronouncements. "I was on a sail boat once. A regatta at the Santa Monica pier. Some guy got me on a boat, you know how it is. TV crew were there. Caught me on film."

Connor thinks Angie has been at the whiskey; she makes no sense. He can smell booze on her.

"What's important about this stone man?" Jackie nods at the map.

"Quilaq is nearby. Sometimes." Frank smiles at Gerry. "You aren't the only one who talks to our friends in the snow. I've been out to the tribes beyond the Kirk Straits. Some say they've seen Quilaq and the stone man on the same horizon."

"Is it far?" Gerry asks. He still sounds doubtful.

Frank shrugs. "Few days walk. Maybe more in this blizzard. We'd do well to pack shelter with us and plenty of food."

"We're going tonight?" Connor looks outside at the thick fall of snow.

"Why not?"

"Yes," Jackie says, urgently. "We've waited long enough to find it."

"Have we, Jackie?" Connor looks at his man. The hair at Jackie's temple is fuzzy and full of static, and he wants to press it down with his tongue. He wants to pull the man to him and wrap his short, squat body around Jackie's waist.

"We have. Ever since Laker's Park, when it could have gone so differently." Jackie catches Connor's fingers and for a second, Connor is shocked. They don't ever touch each other in this way in public. But the group around the table watch them easily, and Hettie is smiling and glancing at Frank in a way that tells Connor she knows about secret love. Jackie goes on. "Do you remember how you dug that hole and we hid in it, and I couldn't eat because they broke my face?

And do you remember boiling corn and making a paste so I could eat?"

"I do, Jackie." Connor squeezes Jackie's fingers.

"You said that one day we'd find somewhere that we could be free to love each other, without a gang chasing us out of town with pitchforks. You said that one day we'd be able to walk down the street, arm in arm, and know we were safe."

"Do you think Quilaq's that place, Jackie?" Gerry asks. He plaits his fingers together, a twist of vines. "Maybe it is. Maybe it's where we can all find the love we need."

"Do you want to know the surest, easiest love of *my* life?" Angie again. Her breasts rest on folded arms, soft, freckled whiteness. "My grandma. I loved that old buzzard and she loved me. I hope I'll meet her again. It's the strangest thing! When Gerry told me about Quilaq, all I could think of was her."

And for all her oddness, Connor feels a squeeze of tenderness towards the bar maid. She has served him beer, chilli and, on one occasion, let him and Jackie sleep in the cellar after a session. He is too far away to touch her, but he smiles, hoping she can feel his love. She seems to; Angie tips her head to one side and smiles back.

"I'm hungry." Ernest puts his nose in the air

and sniffs dramatically. A scent of spiced meat wafts about the bar. "Will there be plenty of food in Quilaq?"

Frank grins, broadly. "There will. I'm sure of that."

And Connor sees Hettie, sitting quietly, her eyes fixed on Frank. She says nothing, not a word, as the group crowd forward and study the map.

Somehow it has been decided that they will leave tonight, even with the snow still falling. When Frank says it will be so, Hettie simply nods and sees the others bow their heads in affirmation. She forgets about the ice splinters in her toes and forgets that her core – that hard centre of her that she always imagines is shaped like a pine cone – has frozen and stuck to her ribs.

No, somehow it has been decided they will set off tonight and those memories of stabbing, awful cold have been wiped away. And now Hettie finds herself in Angie's room, above the bar. She is standing at the end of Angie's un-made bed while the barmaid rummages in a closet, throwing clothes over her shoulder.

"Skirts won't do out in that. You'll need to

change." Angie's disembodied voice from beneath clouds of wool and coats. She slings something across the room Hettie catches it. It is a
suit, the legs sewn in. Hettie has never seen anything like it. The fabric is shiny to touch; water
drips onto it from her still-wet hair and she wipes
it easily away. It does not soak in.

"Waterproof," Angie says, by way of explanation. She is beside Hettie now, and jabs at the
suit with her finger. "Lord knows why I kept the
thing, but it's the best ski suit I ever owned. A
man bought it for me, the one who broke my ribs
in Vancouver." Angie sniffs and looks away
when Hettie sucks her teeth. Facing the window
through which sheets of snow can be seen, she
mutters. "Don't imagine you'd let a man beat on
you that way."

Hettie doesn't know what to say. She can see
Frank's eyes and hands, and his mouth, and
Ernest's happy face nearby. Her mind feels
soaked and damp. She cannot think clearly.

Angie has turned back to the closet and has
produced a pair of jumpers. She hands one to
Hettie and starts to shrug off her clothes. "Layers
would be best. Lots of layers we can take off."

She is not embarrassed about her body and is
suddenly undressed, stripped to her bra. Hettie
stares – she cannot help it. She has never seen

another woman in her underclothes. Angie's ease and confidence astounds her; Hettie has never let Frank see her like that, even in the early days when the excitement of having him near was intoxicating.

But Angie stands stoutly in her room, blotched skin rising in the cool. She tugs on a cotton shirt, lifting up her arms to expose a long, white scar, running from the dip of her armpit almost down to her waist. Hettie gasps and is bewildered to see her own fingers reach out to touch it.

"Snow suit guy." Angie watches Hettie's fingers trail the shiny path down to where it peters out. "He was a real peach."

"Wound like that could have killed you."

Angie sniffs. "Yep. Don't quite know how I pulled through, but he always did say my skin was like leather."

"He sounds delightful."

Angie laughs. "Oh, you have such a prissy way with words, Hettie. He sure was *delightful.*"

Hettie holds Angie's clothes and realises she has to change. There is no privacy. Angie's room is large – it covers most of the floor above the bar – but it's cluttered. A box with a shiny screen sits in the corner, books litter the carpet. Angie has taken to cooking her meals in the room, so there is a makeshift stove pressed against one wall. A sink nearby.

Hettie will have to undress in front of Angie and, wincing, she realises she needs her. The cords on the back of her dress need undoing, or cutting off. She cannot remember the last time she changed her clothes – boiling water to wash in the little shack she shares with Ernest seemed too much trouble.

Angie has scissors in her hands. Without speaking and without Hettie having to ask, she unclips the cord roping the dress to Hettie's body. The material is wet; it peels away from Hettie's back in slippery folds, like fish skin. Hettie shivers as the cold hits her again and Angie pauses, blanket in hand, as Hettie turns round.

"So you are scarred, too," Angie says. Her eyes are on the torn, folded flesh of Hettie's stomach. "Ernest?"

Hettie grabs the blanket and wraps it around herself. She is ashamed of how her body looks, particularly as she can't remember how it got that way.

"Frank says Ernest was cut out, but I can't remember. I was lucky to pull through."

"Like me."

"Like you."

The air in the room seems to warm up a little. Hettie finally looks at Angie, taking in the barmaid's dirty hair and smudged eyes. She imagines her own hair is streaked with filth – she had fallen on the trek over from the shack and had been hauled to her feet by Jackie. A night without sleep or food has added dark shadows to her eyes.

The women are connected. They feel it. Hettie accepts Angie's clothes and puts them on, smelling the dusk of Angie's perfume, feeling the snugness of the snowsuit against her. Angie has surrounded her and, for once, Hettie feels completely peaceful.

"I think," Angie says, her face shining, "I think I am happy you are coming on this journey to find Quilaq. Being with the men is all well and good, but having you come along is...is..."

Hettie catches Angie's hand in her own. "Yes."

Jackie realises he is hungry: he had not stopped to eat Connor's stew before stepping out into the snow and stumbling towards Shay's Bar. The familiar, empty ache blooms in his stomach like it always does, threaded with a line of panic. Will he eat? Will there ever be food?

But Angie and Hettie come down the stairs – Hettie wearing a monstrous pink outfit, the like of which he has never seen before – and Jackie is reminded that he is not at Gillymore now, nor at Laker's Park where he lived in dirt. He is in Stokeland, in Shay's Bar, and there are no men outside with sharp things to stab him with. If he wants to eat, he has a feeling that Angie will provide. The world – his world – has changed in the last few hours, and Jackie feels the community and link with others in the bar in the very fat of his bones.

It is as if Angie has read his thoughts. She smiles dreamily and goes to the little stove at the far end of the bar, and lights a flame underneath a pan. She sets out bowls on the bar, one for each of them. Jackie. Connor. Hettie. Frank. Gerry the Gin. Angie. Little Ernest. The edges of the blue stoneware bowls touch each other companionably. Angie spoons out chilli. The saucepan doesn't seem big enough to hold enough for them all, but it is. Full bowls are passed around.

Jackie takes his and sits with Connor. It feels natural to edge close to his man and stroke the short fellow's cheek before settling down to eat. Again, no one in the bar seems to care.

The snow blows hard outside and thickens the air. Jackie feels they are inside a bubble. As the chilli fills the hole in his stomach and eases his panic, he wants to wrap his arms and legs around Connor and never let go.

Frank is sitting opposite and watches. Round, owl eyes, slow blinks, and Jackie feels his mind unravel. He has told Frank a little of what happened in Gillymore and Laker's Park. He has told Frank about the man who threw the first punch, and that it was the same man who had been inside Jackie's clothes only three days before. Frank had listened as Jackie unburdened himself but offered nothing. Still, Jackie had felt comforted. Cleansed.

Their bowls are empty. Frank stands. The map is in his hands and he has pulled his coat tightly around him. Ernest stands close and Jackie sees the shared blood between father and son; wide space between the eyes, long mouths. Even the identical curl of their hair, stuck tight to their heads. The hum is back in the room again and Jackie feels it deep below his ears, in the funnel between his brain and throat. A coat has been produced from somewhere for Ernst and there are oversized gloves on his hands.

"Would you say we should head for the valley, by way of getting to the Kirk Straits, Gerry?" Frank asks. "Or will the road be unpassable?"

"I should say any road we take will be difficult," Gerry says. "Whether we walk through the valley or take the long way north and then loop west – we'll face the weather each and every way. There's something else, though, that troubles me more."

"Oh?"

Jackie feels the breath stop in his throat; the pressure inside the bubble grows.

"Frank, this talk of an enormous stone man confuses me." It is an effort for Gerry to speak. Pride lines the crevices of his face; he has taken the narrow tracks and ruts of the earth around Stokeland into his skin. "I've never come across it."

"It's there," Frank says, smoothly. "It's a kind of marker, I believe, between the soft ground around Stokeland and the unknown tundra beyond."

"And yet I've never seen this marker, and I've tramped these parts for longer than I can remember." Desperation creeps into Gerry's voice. "How is that so?"

"Ray Sullivan may have passed it," Frank says. He moves the map and the paper rustles. "He is a man that moves easily around these parts, easier than all of us. One moment he's at Tramper's Creek, the next he's as far south as Yellowknife. I don't quite know how he does it. I've never found been able to leave Stokeland so effortlessly, but he sure does have a way. I hope he turns up while we're on this journey or we find him along the way."

"We're going to set off anyway?" Connor asks. He is holding his boots over a small box nailed to the wall, a box that belches out hot air. It is an ingenious invention, Jackie thinks, and watches as Connor slides the boots back onto his feet, a look of pleasure folding over the small man's face as his feet are warmed.

"We are leaving, yes." There is no question or argument. Frank speaks simply and with authority. "Gather yourselves and whatever you're taking. We're heading out."

The bar door is thrown open – it seems an appropriate, dramatic gesture, now they are finally leaving. Connor feels as though it has taken forever to get to this point – he feels a pull behind his belly button towards the open door and pressure in his calves to move, his body throbbing forward. Snow swirls in unremittingly. Connor steadies himself and holds a scarf to his face. Instinctively, he looks for Jackie. His man is nearby, stepping out into the white with an assuredness that startles Connor. It is as though Jackie knows where he is going, though none of them really do.

Connor's legs move, and Angie is behind him. He wonders for a moment what Paul Shay will say when he comes to open the bar and finds his barmaid gone. And all of the chilli eaten. Angie looks up at Connor, and he senses her thoughts. She smiles brightly. He feels it, too – happiness, joy, in the lining of his heart. Unmistakeable and bewildering.

The snow is thick and peaked in drifts, but the group stays together. Jackie leads the way, Frank just behind him. Ernest is between Angie and Hettie, and Connor sees how one of the women has a hand on the child's shoulder at all times. Then there comes Gerry and himself. They wade towards the edge of town and, without a glance behind at the bar and the store and the carpenter's, step off into the blizzard.

They laugh as they do.

It is not long before Connor stumbles. His legs are not built for walking long distances, but Gerry is beside him in an instant. Hettie helps Ernest stand, too. Jackie has his arm on Frank's elbow, dragging him up. They cannot see but they feel their way along, sensing each other, feeling the hum again, the hum that united them in the bar.

Connor cannot remember straying this far from town before. He knows his route, to the mine, back to the rooms above the carpenter's, the path to the store. He does not know this part of Stokeland, out beyond the border. The happiness leaks a little from his heart and he turns to look back, but the buildings are already hidden. There is no choice now – they have to press on.

They walk and stumble and fall and get to their feet, and walk again. Amidst the billows and swirls it is impossible to tell how long they have been going. Connor knows his coat is wet but he doesn't feel cold, not like before when they made their way over to Shay's Bar. The chilli sits in his belly, warming him through.

At some point they sleep. Connor has a moment of fear and wonder – it is foolish to lay down in the snow. Even he, who grew up in a land of dust and heat, knows lying down in the snow to rest is a bad idea. But the group does it without question. Frank digs out a hole with his hands. Jackie helps him. Before long they have built a shelter, a circle into which they all fit. They shape the sides to rise up so they curve over their bodies and the centre is open to the sky. Gerry lights a fire, producing flint and kindling from a bag wrapped inside his coat, and Angie has food. Just plain biscuits, but there's enough to go round. They all eat their fill and lie down. Jackie bends his body behind Connor, his long legs scooped around Connor's shorter ones. No one says anything or judges them. They all wish each other goodnight and, before long they are all asleep. And still it snows.

When they wake it is morning and Connor is hot. The fire has burned down to embers and snow has fallen on the arched walls of the shelter. It is as though the group is in a white, warm womb. The others stir, all waking at around the same time. Frank sits up – he has been holding Ernest all night and flexes his arm, ruefully, cramp making him wince. His fingers finally working, he spreads out the map and he and Gerry crouch over it, muttering.

Angie has a kettle on the go – where it came from, Connor doesn't know, but there's coffee before long and Connor feels hotter than ever. He starts to shrug off his coat when Jackie stops him. "Don't," Jackie says. "As soon as we step outside, you'll freeze."

He's right. It is icy and raw beyond the shelter. As they pack up and leave, Connor looks back at the little mound regretfully – it has given them protection and comfort. He does not know where they are headed.

But they make another shelter that night, in much the same way. And one the night after. They march further away from Stokeland, miles away now, and Frank seems more confident the Stoneman of the map is close by.

They see very little on their travels. The trees thin out until they are on bare tundra, snow falling even here. The air is wadded and still; Connor can't hear the call of a bird or the drum of an animal. He wonders how Gerry made a living out here and what possible creature he was able to trap. The group stay close together, filling each other's footsteps. Occasionally Ernest chatters, cheerfully, about whatever thought is in his head. Connor is becoming fond of the boy and his sweet stubbornness. They hold hands from time to time, Connor pulling the child on.

And then around noon of the fourth day, Frank stops. He is in the lead as usual, with Jackie behind him. He holds the map in his hands as he always does. They all stop, crowding together. The sun is pale yellow in the sky and Connor thinks ice will form on his tongue if he pokes it out. He does, just to see, winking at Ernest and making the boy giggle.

"What is it, Frank?" Jackie asks.

Frank frowns. He is not looking at the map but is staring out in the distance. "There. To the west. Can you see it?"

Connor strains but, as a small man, it is difficult for him to see the horizon. He edges to the side of the group, to get a clear view.

Jackie gasps. Gerry, too. Connor looks again. What is it? What have they seen?

Then Hettie and Angie both make a sound, a high-pitched squeal. Hettie has her hands to her mouth.

"What is it?" Connor asks, exasperatedly. He still cannot see a thing and feels excluded. But then Ernest tugs at his hand.

The boy pulls him down to his level. Ernest is grinning, widely, loveably. "Look, Connor. It's there!"

And then Connor sees it. Standing grey and still, a shape. A man made of stone. The Stoneman of Frank's map.

It takes hours to reach the Stoneman and, when they do, night is falling and the temperature has dropped. The group are aware of the stiffening breeze and the occasional shard of ice across their teeth, but they don't feel the cold as viscerally as they might. They stand beside the Stoneman. It soars into the air, standing so tall that Angie can't see the top.

She leans back, feeling the bones of her old, tired neck pop. How can I not have seen this before? she thinks, and laughs at the wonder of it.

The others laugh, too. The monument is so massive. Clouds gather above. A lone bird calls out in the distance but the sound is muffled and wadded against the stone.

"Am I dreaming this?" Gerry the Gin says and he rubs his eyes. Angie feels sorry for him; she supposes he feels embarrassed. All this time, walking and trapping in the tundra, guiding men who drink in Shay's Bar and speak of heading north or south. She has heard him, offering advice as to which route to take and which to avoid. And he had no knowledge of this Stoneman. How could he have missed it? How could any of them have missed it?

Hettie is kneeling down next to Ernest and pulling his coat about him, though the gesture seems to come more from habit than necessity. Ernest's cheeks are rosy. Angie feels hot, too, the warmest since leaving Stokeland. She reaches out, tentatively, and puts a hand on the rock of the Stoneman. Odd images flash in front of her eyes – her grandmother, shelling peas in a wicker chair, the smell of menthol – and the rock is warm.

"We should stay here for the night," Frank says. He sets down his backpack. "We can study the map again, now we've found the Stoneman."

"Or he found you." A voice in the mist, not one of the group. Angie swings round quickly, a sliver of alarm stretching across her belly. They all look around, confusion in their faces. Who could be here, now, all this way out?

And then a man walks around the side of the Stoneman. He is wearing a long trench coat and carries a smart briefcase, hilariously inappropriate for such an environment. Angie hoots with laughter. It is Ray Sullivan.

"You old devil!" and she runs to him. She feels joyously pleased to see him and throws her arms around his neck. It is the first time she has ever embraced him and, as she presses her cheek against his rough, whiskery skin, she thinks Ray is like all the men she has ever slept with: a little seedy, doused in aftershave. A player. She glances back at Hettie and sees the other woman has felt longing, too.

"What the hell, Ray…" and Jackie is beside him, too, pumping the man's hand. Connor, as well, slapping the salesman on the back. They all gather around him, and they see his smart shoes, tailored trousers.

"There's a settlement a few miles north of here," Ray says, by way of explanation. "And one just a mile south. You must have walked past it. I have an appointment there."

"We hoped we'd find you," Frank says. His round eyes take in the scene.

"And I wondered whom I might meet on my travels. I do come across groups such as yours, from time to time." Ray bends over and pops open his briefcase. He takes out a hipflask, sips, and passes it round. They all drink, even Ernest.

"You've walked everywhere," Frank says. "You know where roads lead that we don't know exist." Frank leans over and touches the Stoneman. "We didn't even know this was here."

Gerry coughs and shuffles his feet. Angie feels the tang of sympathy for him and slips her hand into his own. Ernest is holding on to Connor again, who edges against Jackie. Hettie links her fingers into the crook of Frank's elbow; they are all touching each other again, forming a circle, in the middle of which stands Ray.

Ray looks at them all in turn, taking his time. "What are you looking for? What on earth can have enticed you all the way out here, where even the snow is afraid to fall?" But he is smiling as he asks. Angie sees that he knows already.

"Quilaq," she says, softly. "And you know where it is."

A hum; a low drone. The sound is back. Angie feels it fuzzing behind her bellybutton and the sensation is joyous and wonderful. She flexes up on her tiptoes, lifted up by it.

"Of course I know," Ray says.

They are crying now, as one. Silent, easy tears flow. Ernest drops Connor's hand and tugs on Ray's coat. "Will you take us, mister?"

Ray grins down. His teeth are yellow and filmy; he is a drinker. But he nods. "Of course. It should be easy now we are all together."

They are ready to go and Jackie thinks – this is it, we're really off. But Ernest stumbles; Connor catches him. Ray pauses.

So they turn back to the Stoneman and Jackie unfurls a rug. There is no shelter, but the group doesn't miss it. He and Connor sit down, warm as toast. Gerry lights a fire and they all circle it, near to the Stoneman. Angie fishes out a cooking pot from a bag, Ray takes out a couple of hares, wrapped in brown paper, from his briefcase of surprises. Gerry skins them quickly, accepts the skewers Ray offers and roasts the animals over the fire. Soon a tasty, rich smell fills the air and Jackie feels hungry for the first time in days.

Ernest is drawing circles in the snow and Jackie sees that the boy's finger has become white with cold. He leans over and folds his hand gently over the child's. "Let's not lose them, eh?" he says and the boy grins, dreamily.

He feels Connor lean against him and his man's breathing slows; Connor is tired. Ray grins over and Jackie feels momentarily unsure. Since leaving Stokeland he has slept beside Connor, legs tangled together just as they might in their private space, and they've held hands when sitting around the fire. No one has muttered or moved away. Jackie has felt acceptance like he has never experienced before. Now, with Ray smiling so openly, he takes pause. Had Ray seen their closeness back in Stokeland, in Shay's Bar?

"Paul Shay's place isn't like most others," Ray says. "All kinds of folk have gathered at Shay's, one time or another."

Jackie is shocked, and it takes all of his control just to nod. His forehead feels pulled back, as though Ray has opened his skull and rummaged around in his brain. There is a taste of spice on the air and the smell of strong, gamey meat.

"But I bet if you stopped to think about it, you can only remember these folk at Paul's bar," Ray says, waving at the group, sitting quietly and starting into the fire. "They won't all have been there at the same time - not before you left to find Quilaq, but you remember them."

Jackie thinks. Ray is right. He has drunk with Connor, of course, and been served by Angie. Frank has held fort at the bar, entrancing all comers with his stories, though the faces of those listening are grainy and blurred, and Jackie can't see through the fog to identify them. Gerry the Gin has slumped over the bar from time to time. Even Hettie has come in on odd occasions, looking for her man. But never Ernest. And never the group together.

Ray chuckles. "That's right. Never all together until tonight. Paul's bar is a place where, when the right group come together, magic happens."

"And you know this how?" Angie pipes up. Jackie didn't think she was listening; she is sitting next to Hettie and they are whispering and giggling together, as they have done these past days. Jackie and Connor have marvelled at it. The companionship between the women is unexpected and deep. Jackie was sure they hated each other before, before they started on this quest.

Ray leans over and helps Gerry turn the hares over above the fire. "I've travelled all about this land selling solar panels. Shining a light. I've met enough people to know magic when I see it."

Hettie snorts. "I've heard about the sort of people you met."

A chill descends and Jackie shivers. The low hum, the one that seems to sit beneath his ears when they are all together, fades away. The corners of Ray's mouth turn down.

"And you heard that from my wife, I suppose?" he asks. "Can you remember her name?"

Hettie falters. She edges against Angie, seeking comfort. "For the life of me, I cannot."

"Then it doesn't matter." Ray spreads out his hands. "We're here, together, right now, at this place. That's what matters. Gerry, I think those are ready."

The hares are cooked and Ray strips meat from their bones, not appearing to be bothered by the heat of the animals' flesh. Meat is put in the pot and the group gather round, sitting even closer than before.

Angie takes a piece of meat and chews, contentedly. She laughs, softly. "In all my life, I've never felt amongst such friends."

Jackie feels tears prick the backs of his eyes. He is usually uncomfortable around such sentiment. He doesn't like to hear Connor say he loves him. But Angie speaks honestly and cleanly and he believes her.

"I hope when we find Quilaq I will be with you still," Angie says and her eyes shine.

"Yes," Gerry says, quietly. "I hope to find someone to love." He glances at Angie and a warm zip links the group.

"And you, Hettie?" Ray asks. He has a skewer in his hand and points it at her, as though he is conducting an orchestra.

"Frank," she says. "I will be there with Frank."

"And I will have a belly full of food!" Frank says, slapping his stomach. They all laugh and he turns his moon-like eyes on them. "To never starve again would be a fine thing."

"Connor?" Ray twists the skewer to point at Jackie's man.

"I'll be with Jackie," Connor says. No blush, no bluster. His twisted little legs edge next to Jackie.

Eyes turn to Jackie and he winces, momentarily, a worm of fear crawling through his skull – they will beat Connor and I, now they know. They will beat us for being deviants.

But there are smiles all round – even Ernest is grinning, happily.

Jackie knows that what he has to say might puncture the warm bubble they have created, but he has to say it. "I hope I can be free in Quilaq," he says. "I have hidden who I am for so long. I want to be free to be with anyone I want."

He wonders if Connor will move his leg away, but he doesn't.

"And Ernest?" Hettie asks. "What do you wish to find in Quilaq, Ernest?"

The child doesn't answer but eats. Hettie stares at her child. Eating. Another wonder.

Ray laughs. "He is the key. He will lead you to Quilaq."

They spend the night beside the Stoneman and when they wake, Frank finds his hands inside Hettie's clothes, cupping her breasts as she sleeps on. He is shocked but fights the urge to flinch away. He blinks rapidly. He has not held Hettie in this way, not ever. Their transactions in the past have been brief and resentful, almost as if they disliked their physical need for each other.

But Hettie feels so warm and right under his

hands. His body doesn't stir, not as it might, as she murmurs and moves a little, pressing back into him, breasts slipping across his palm; instead a feeling of completeness steals over him and he nestles closer, pushing his mouth against the nape of her neck.

When he wakes again, the rest of the group are up and about and Hettie has wriggled round to face him. She is looking at him, curiously, his hands about her bare waist, inside the awful pink outfit she wears. He can tell she is wondering what has happened and why he is holding her so, and he sees his woman fight her natural inclination to lash out and push him away. But there has been a shift within her, too, and she simply pushes the length of her body against the length of his. Neither of them care who sees – they hold each other.

A gentle nudge on his foot – Connor. The toady little man is grinning, sheepishly. "Sorry, you looked too peaceful to disturb. But Ray says it's time to start out for Quilaq and there's snow coming."

Frank sits up and looks at the horizon. He can see further than the others and picks out blue snow clouds a few hours in the distance.

"Let's move," he says. "That's not just snow, but a storm."

He still has the ability to captivate the group and they move immediately upon his bidding. But Ray leads them, not Frank. Frank can hear the familiar hum in his ears and he steps into the tracks left by Jackie and Gerry. He doesn't mind that Ray leads the way – the man knows how to get to Quilaq, after all. In fact, he feels lighter than he ever has, now that the group also looks to Ray for answers.

He finds Hettie's hand linked in his, and reaches out to take the flailing hand of his son. Ernest finds it harder going than the others, being small and the snow being thick, so Frank shoves the boy in front of him, into the steps already taken.

They march on and the storm descends. Soon it is impossible to see each other and they stop, calling to each other in laughing whoops. Gerry produces a rope and they lash themselves together. The rope seems endless, long enough for them to tie it round their waists. They stumble on, still warm, still connected and, Frank realises joyfully, he is still full from the meal the night before.

In the end they cannot make it through the snow so they gather together in a tight circle. Ray won't let them sit down. "The snow will pass," he says, though Frank can't see how that can be true – the sky is thick and white. The snow heaps over their shoulders and Frank pushes Ernest in the middle. The boy smiles round at their hot faces; they have become a turret and he is at their centre.

And then the snow stops, just as Ray says it will. Frank lifts up his head and shakes away the flakes. The rest do the same, rebirthing.

Ray points to a gathering of trees. "We go that way. The walking will be easier, under cover. We'll get to Quilaq before you know it."

He is right. The going is easier. Frank can't remember the forest on his map and puzzles a little as he walks. But Ray sets off purposefully. His briefcase swings at his side and Ernest walks with him, giggling, pointing at clumps of snow falling from branches.

They must have walked for several hours for Frank's feet start to pinch and Connor has fallen behind. The man's bowed legs arch painfully as he pushes forward. Jackie has his elbow and helps him along. The men touch each other with an ease and simplicity that makes a lump come to Frank's throat.

Ray is talking as they walk. They are threaded out but the words carry and they can all hear; it is though his words weave into the ever-present hum linking them together.

"You didn't really need me to find Quilaq," he says. "Nobody does, but they don't believe it. The people I've led to this place! I'm supposed to be selling solar panels but all I seem to do is find people who are lost and take them where they want to go. I must walk the length of the tundra, picking up stragglers. They always want to find Quilaq."

Frank listens and watches Ray. The man seems to talk to himself more than them, but his words are comforting and the trees slip by as they march on.

"You all know about the place, deep down," Ray says. "It's deep in your bones. Some of you are reminded of people you once loved when you say the word -" and here he waves to Angie, gamely struggling on – "and others think of food or water or comfort. Ah, here we are."

Frank almost misses it – did Ray say they were here? "Where, Ray? You don't mean Quilaq?"

Ray nods. The group work their way through the last of the trees and come to stand beside him. The rope still ties them, connecting them as they stand in a line and look in the direction that Ray points.

They have exited the forest and are standing at the edge of a field. Lights shine in the distance.

Frank sniffs: he can smell baking and bread, and spices on the wind. Someone is singing.

"Is this Quilaq?" he asks. He feels the pinch of tears and squeezes his eyes shut. When he looks around, he sees the others are crying, too.

"Of course it is. Always has been." Ray waves an arm out. "There's a place where you can gather, where you'll be welcomed as newcomers. You'll know it when you see it. But this is as far as I go. One of you will have to lead the rest of you there. One of you is perfect for the task."

And then, inexplicably, Ernest starts to laugh.

Ray drops his hand on Ernest's shoulder and the boy looks up at him. What a beautiful, gap-toothed little thing, Ray thinks. How perfect for the task he is.

Ray points across the snow-covered field. There is a building in the distance, a sliver of cracked light breaking through the darkness. "That's where you need to go," Ray says. "Walk over to the door and knock. Someone will let you in."

"Why can't I go with him?" Hettie asks. She

is curious, not anxious. She looks at her child, bemused at how straight his back is, how determined he seems though, of course, giggles still burst from him.

"It requires innocence to find your way to Quilaq," Ray says. "It's one of the rules. I can't explain it, and it isn't necessary for you to know more. And whom among you is more innocent than the child?"

A few snickers. Angie is thinking of a man she spent a summer with, without the knowledge of his wife, and Gerry the Gin is thinking of money, taken from an unattended wallet left on a bar. The thoughts wash through them and they are left with the sense that no, they are not innocent exactly. Then the memories disappear and they can't remember what they were thinking about.

"Go," says Ray, giving Ernest a gentle push, and Ernest sets off across the field. The snow comes up to his knees but he doesn't stop.

The group watch him and they hold their breath. For the first time in days they can feel the cold again and, when Ernest reaches the door and knocks, they exhale together. Warm air escapes from their bodies, spiralling into the night in white clouds.

The door opens; Ernest stands in a glare of

light. The silhouette of a man falls across him. It is a huge, big man. He fills the space between the field and building and looks down at the child on his hearth. Then he motions Ernest in and, stepping to the side, the light casts over his face.

The watching group gasp and it is Jackie who says it first. "That's Paul Shay!"

They turn to look at each other, confused. "How can it be Paul?" Connor says. "Has he made it to Quilaq?"

But Ray is backing away, unwilling to answer questions. A serene smile fixed on his face. He is turning back to the trees.

"Wait!" Angie tries to catch his arm but Ray melts from her grasp.

Then Paul's voice booms across the field. "Come on. If you want to make it, move those legs of yours."

They do, but each in the group is wearing a frown. It doesn't take long to cross the field and soon they are standing in front of the huge meaty slab that is Paul Shay. He has wild red hair and shoulders that seem to go on forever. He grins at them all and nods when he sees Angie.

"Welcome," he says and swings back the door.

Warm spiced air; a wooden bar; glass lined up. Hettie gasps. The group glance at each other.

"We're back at your bar," Gerry says. His voice is small, as though he is frightened to say what he sees.

"There must be some mistake," Jackie mutters. He glares at Paul, who is now chuckling to himself.

"It is my bar, yes" the bear of a man says.

They step into the room. Ernest is spinning in a circle, arms outstretched. When the group nears, he stops, laughing loudly. "We made it, we made it!"

"But we're back in Stokeland!" Angie hisses.

Paul Shay is now behind the bar and pouring liquid into shot glasses. There is one for each of them. Angie. Gerry. Hettie. Frank. Jackie. Connor. Even Ernest. The bottle is not one they've ever seen more and the fluid tipped into glasses is thick, more like honey than whiskey.

"Did Ray leave you at the trees?" Paul shoves the glasses forward with his fat fingers.

"He wouldn't answer our questions," Connor says.

Paul snorts. He sweats into the room, the smell of worked, toiled flesh wafting out. "He doesn't have all the answers. His work is to bring people here. Now. Drink."

They eye the yellow liquid dubiously and

Paul motions with his hand, encouragingly. "Drink."

They drink. The fluid is warm and comforting and tastes differently to each of them. To Angie, it tastes of homemade lemonade, bittersweet. Gerry tastes broth and the heavy tang of ale. Jackie tastes coffee, Connor deep red wine. Frank tastes stout and Hettie tastes hot tea. Ernest smacks his lips. "I love milk!"

"Paul, why are we back here?" Jackie asks. "We've walked for days, all the way out to the Stoneman. How is it that we're back in your bar?"

"Is this Quilaq?" Frank says, suddenly. He places his glass back down on the bar and turns to look at Paul, squarely in the face. It isn't easy, given the size of the bar owner, and Frank has to stand on his tiptoes.

Paul humpfs again. The sound is guttural. "These are the best times for me. When new people make it."

Angie shakes her head. "You've known me for years, Paul. I'm hardly new."

"You're in Stokeland and Quilaq," Paul says. He waves a hand around the bar. "There are places like this out in the snow – little towns, cut off from the world. None of you, none of you remember how you got here, do you?"

They all think, brows furrowed. Not one can remember the exact time they arrived in Stokeland.

"Each of you made it here after a time of great danger." Paul looks at each of them in turn. "Angie, there was the man who broke your ribs and cut your throat. Hettie and Ernest – at the child's birth. Gerry, you've spent nights exposed in the cold, too many of them. And Frank. You've owed too many angry men too much money. As for Jackie and Connor – well, the time at Laker's Park was hard."

The group is silent, distant in their memories.

"That's what you went through to get here," Paul says. "And finding Quilaq means different things for each of you. Each of you want to find something – that one thing – that will make your heart stop aching and your mind rest. Am I right?"

They glance at each other. Paul, with his barking voice and fierce way of speaking, is right.

He nods, satisfied. "Finding Quilaq means different things to every soul here. Every last one of them who makes it to Stokeland."

There is a noise in the room and they look around; suddenly they see people in the bar. In fact, the bar is bustling. Tables are full, booths are taken. But the figures are blurred and, try as they might, the group can't pick out the faces in the crowd.

"You'll be able to see them clearly soon," Paul says, as though he can read their thoughts. "Once the drink and understanding has settled in."

"You said there are other places like Quilaq," Connor says, tentatively.

Paul nods. "Isn't it wonderful?"

"But...how?" Frank knows what he wants to ask but, oddly for him, he cannot find the words.

Paul catches hold of a hand next to him; Hettie's. Automatically the group link up, fingers entwined, until they stand in a linked circle.

"You found your way to Quilaq by finding each other," Paul says. "Stokeland is a holding place. A breath. And when you find each other, you exhale."

And they do. Their breath funnels out and they hear the hum again.

"What does Ray do?" Gerry asks.

Paul sighs and they can see he is thinking, contemplating how best to answer. "The thing is, you can only leave Stokeland and set off for Quilaq when the shape of you is right. By that I mean that you have the right group. Like you have now – you needed to come together in order to find Quilaq. You bring different things to each other; I can't explain what, just as I can't explain what love is. But when you came together, here, in this bar, as it always happens in Stokeland, you were ready to leave and walk to the Stoneman. Ray's job is to meet you there and guide you here."

"Solar panels," Angie murmurs. "I thought he sold solar panels."

Paul bares his crooked grin, his mouth crammed with broken teeth. "He shines a light. When the time is right for him, he will find his own Quilaq."

Someone bustles by and a drink is spilled. Paul turns and shouts over his shoulder, and a face appears. A man's red, whiskey-soaked face – they can see him clearly now. He tips a hat in Paul's direction and bends down to mop up the spillage with the arm of his coat.

"What now?" Frank asks.

Paul expands his hands. "Now you find peace, here. You won't ever be hungry or cold or empty of love. You've found each other and found Quilaq."

"Like these people?" Angie asks, indicating to the bar.

"Exactly."

The bar is crammed now; they feel the press

of others against them and hot happiness in the room. Each person rings with gladness. Angie melts into the memory of her grandmother; Gerry slips his hand into the bar maid's, hope and love ignited within. Hettie and Frank embrace, with Ernest between them, whole and strong. And Conner wraps himself around Jackie, as his man leans casually against him.

Paul Bay stands back and looks at the group, another group safely together. The snow gathers again outside Stokeland but here, in the bar at Quilaq, the light shines on.

Dear reader,

We hope you enjoyed reading *Quilaq*. Please take a moment to leave a review, even if it's a short one. Your opinion is important to us.

Discover more books by Rebecca Burns at https://www.nextchapter.pub/authors/rebecca-burns

Want to know when one of our books is free or discounted? Join the newsletter at http://eep-url.com/bqqB3H

Best regards,
Rebecca Burns and the Next Chapter Team

You could also like:
A Matter of Latitude by Isobel Blackthorn

To read the first chapter for free, please head to:
https://www.nextchapter.pub/books/a-matter-
of-latitude-thriller-set-in-spain

ABOUT THE AUTHOR

Rebecca Burns is an award-winning short-story writer and novelist. Two of her story collections have been long-listed for the Edge Hill Short Story Prize, the UK's only award for short story collections. She lives in Leicestershire with her young family. *Quilaq* is her sixth published work of fiction.

Other works by Rebecca Burns
Short Story Collections
Catching the Barramundi (long-listed for Edge Hill)
The Settling Earth (long-listed for Edge Hill)
Artefacts and Other Stories

Novels – historical fiction
The Bishop's Girl
Beyond the Bay

Lightning Source UK Ltd.
Milton Keynes UK
UKHW040421171220
375384UK00001B/64

9 781034 033523